"Stay away from the hoodoo man."

"Why do you think I wear this dime? To keep hoodoo away, that's why."

Streaks of fear ran down Clara's back. *"You said it was for headaches."* Why hadn't Momma told her the truth about the dime a long time ago? Momma keeping it a secret made it more frightening.

"Daddy didn't want me scaring you girls." Momma gave a short laugh. *"But you can get a fix put on you anytime, Clara. Anytime. You got to be careful."*

"How does the dime keep hoodoo away?"

"Anybody tries to put a fix on us, the dime will tarnish, turn dark gray."

Momma peered at the dime. *"Still bright. Now listen to me, Clara. There's plenty of good reason to stay away from the hoodoo man."*

"What reason, Momma?"

"Ain't for children to know."

OTHER PUFFIN BOOKS YOU MAY ENJOY

Elizabeth Partridge

Clara and the Hoodoo Man

PUFFIN BOOKS

PUFFIN BOOKS
Published by the Penguin Group
Penguin Putnam Inc., 375 Hudson Street, New York, New York 10014, U.S.A.
Penguin Books Ltd, 27 Wrights Lane, London W8 5TZ, England
Penguin Books Australia Ltd, Ringwood, Victoria, Australia
Penguin Books Canada Ltd, 10 Alcorn Avenue, Toronto, Ontario, Canada M4V 3B2
Penguin Books (N.Z.) Ltd, 182-190 Wairau Road, Auckland 10, New Zealand

Penguin Books Ltd, Registered Offices: Harmondsworth, Middlesex, England

First published in the United States of America by Dutton Children's Books,
a division of Penguin Books USA Inc., 1996
Published in Puffin Books, 1998

1 3 5 7 9 10 8 6 4 2

THE LIBRARY OF CONGRESS HAS CATALOGED THE DUTTON EDITION AS FOLLOWS:
Partridge, Elizabeth.
Clara and the hoodoo man/by Elizabeth Partridge.—1st ed.
p. cm.
Summary: In 1900, Clara always seems to find ways to worry her mother
in their home near Red Owl Mountain, Tennessee, but when her
younger sister is near death, Clara risks seeking the help of the
herbal healer her mother calls a hoodoo man.
ISBN 0-525-45403-9 (hardcover)
[1. Mountain life—Tennessee–Fiction. 2. Afro-Americans—Fiction.
3. Sisters—Fiction. 4. Tennessee—Fiction.] I. Title.
PZ7.P26C1 1996 [Fic]—dc20 96-674 CIP AC

Puffin Books ISBN 0-14-038348-4

Printed in the United States of America

For my mother,
Elizabeth Woolpert Partridge

Trouble is seasoning.

Persimmons ain't good till they're frostbit.

Old African-American saying

chapter one

Clara eased the door open a crack and peered out. She saw the sharp blue sky. She saw the bright red flowers of Momma's bee balm planted around the porch. Nothing moving anywhere. Good.

She pushed the door open a few more inches. Now she could see the field and, past that, the willows, their gnarly roots holding tight to the creek banks. Smack in the middle of the creek stood Momma, up to her knees in water. She was bent over, washing out a big earthenware crock. Momma wouldn't know a thing till she was done.

Clara slipped out onto the porch, letting the door shut quietly behind her. Then she dropped so gently to her hands and knees it was like a puff of wind knocked her down. Slowly, barely breathing, she crawled across the splintery wood. She was careful to stay hidden behind the three crocks Momma had set out to dry.

Clara stared through the bee balm. There they were. Past Momma's garden, down in front of the barn. And none of them looking her way. She let out a deep breath.

The whole chicken flock was pecking and scratching in the dust. There weren't many now—just a dozen hens and a rooster. One night about a month ago, a weasel had dug into the henhouse and bit the heads off six or seven chickens before Daddy could scare it away.

Clara looked carefully at the flock. She spotted her favorite hen, Blackberry, right next to the rooster. Blackberry's feathers glinted green as she stretched her wings in the morning sun. She gave a sudden shake, then snapped them shut and peered nervously around with dark yellow eyes.

"Blackberry, you're nothing but natural-born trouble," Clara whispered to herself. "Soon as you head off into the bushes, I'm going to follow you."

Every day for a week, Blackberry had been sneaking off and laying an egg in her hidden nest. Then she would run back to the flock and cry out *Ca-da! Ca-da!* Clara knew as soon as Blackberry had laid eight or ten eggs, she'd settle down and go broody, sitting on those eggs day and night till they hatched. Good way to get herself killed.

Clara had to find those eggs and move them into the henhouse. Once a weasel got your chickens, it would come back every night, trying to get in again. The hen house was safe now, because Daddy had boarded up the hole the weasel had made. But if Blackberry was out in the field, she wouldn't stand a chance. Just the thought of a weasel sinking its sharp teeth into Blackberry made Clara shiver.

The door banged shut and her little sister, Bessie, came up next to her.

"Hush!" Clara hissed.

"I didn't say anything."

Blackberry snapped her head toward the porch and stared straight at Bessie.

Clara sighed and rose from her hiding place.

"What are you doing?" asked Bessie.

"Watching Blackberry. She's sneaking off and laying her eggs somewhere. I was going to follow her to her nest."

"I'll help."

"You're too noisy, Bessie. She'll never sneak off with you around." Besides, Clara wanted to find Blackberry's nest on her own to surprise Momma. She'd be mighty proud of Clara, bringing the hen and her eggs in where they'd be safe. Blackberry was their best broody hen, raising up two or three nestfuls of bitties each year. And they sure did need new chicks now.

"Momma says four eyes are better than two," said Bessie defiantly.

"I said no." Clara sat down on the edge of the porch, next to the crocks. She dangled her bare feet in the bee balm. Blackberry had turned around and was scratching in the dust.

Clara looked away from the chickens. She traced the big blue number 10 glazed on the side of the crock. Momma thought a good ten-gallon crock was better than a barrel, because it would never rot out. "You take care of it, it will last forever," she had said this morning when she started washing the crocks.

Splashing came from the creek. Momma was scrubbing the last crock, her arms dark against the pale container.

"Then let's go frog gigging in the creek," said Bessie.

"You can only go frog gigging at night," replied Clara.

She hated wading out in the muddy water and stabbing those helpless little frogs with her gigging stick. They squirmed terribly till they died. But she wasn't about to say so to Bessie. Hardly anything bothered Bessie. She'd even go to the outhouse at night when it was pitch black. Clara always used a candle stub out of the cigar box she kept under her bed.

"Why don't you go help Momma?" she told Bessie.

"I don't want to. Anyway, she's all done."

Clara watched as Momma started up the path from the creek. She was barefoot, her long skirt tucked up into her waistband, her arms wrapped tight around the crock.

"Let's climb the elm tree and see who goes highest," said Bessie.

"No." Bessie was only in her fives, but she was mighty good at climbing.

"Let's walk the log across the creek."

Clara shook her head. Lately Bessie seemed to turn everything into a challenge. "Momma will blame me if you fall off."

"I never fall off."

Clara knew that was true. She hated to step forward unless she was holding on to one of the branches that stuck out. But Bessie always seemed to run right across.

"Maybe later." Clara brushed her bare feet through the bee balm and took a big breath of the sweet smell. The bees working in Momma's garden filled the air with a peaceful hum. This was Clara's favorite time of the year. It seemed like the whole world just stood still for days, warm and waiting. Then it let out a big sigh as winter came sweeping in. There'd be three months of school, with a fire in the schoolhouse stove, and her friend Annie Mae sitting next to her on the bench, and roasted sweet potatoes stuck in the fire for dinner. And Bessie still too little to go to school.

Momma pushed in between two of the bee-balm plants and eased the crock onto the porch.

"There, that's the last one," she said. "Now I'm ready for the killing frost."

The killing frost—to Clara, it seemed like a sad name. There'd be a few light frosts, then a hard freeze that would turn Momma's garden brown, even the bright red bee balm. But the worst part was that Daddy would butcher the hog. He'd put the hams and shoulders and middlings in the hollowed-out log behind the house, covering them carefully with wood chips. Momma would make the scraps into sausage with red pepper and sage. She'd fill the crocks, pouring boiling-hot lard on top to seal them. In the dark gray-brown time of winter, Momma would break through the lard on top and fry up the sausages. Clara loved to eat them, even though she hated the butchering.

"Are you done down at the barn, Clara?"

"Yes'm." Soon as Blackberry wasn't paying her no never-mind, she'd be on her again like fleas on a dog.

Momma shook out her skirt. The dime hanging around her neck caught the sun and sent out soft sparkles of light. She said the dime kept headaches away. When the headaches did come, she rubbed salt into wild peach leaves and put them on her forehead.

"Sweeping done, Lil Bits?" Momma called Bessie by her nickname.

"Yes'm."

"When I get done inside, we'll get the sage and start drying it for the sausage."

"But Momma . . ." Clara hesitated. If she told Momma she wanted to find Blackberry's nest, Momma would make her take Bessie, sure as gravy.

"Push those crocks back against the wall, Clara. That'll get them out of harm's way," said Momma. "Then you can play with Bessie."

Clara stared at the porch. Now she'd never be able to shake off her sister.

"You hear me, Clara? I said to play nice with Bessie."

"Yes'm." Clara looked up as Momma went into the house.

"Why don't we catch grasshoppers?" said Bessie. "We can throw them in webs and watch the spiders wrap them up and bite them."

Clara didn't much like it when the grasshoppers spit tobacco juice on her hands. And it made her feel sick watching them struggle helplessly to get away.

"Remember," said Bessie, "you're supposed to play nice with me." She grinned at Clara.

"I got to move the crocks," Clara muttered. She grabbed hold of one and dragged it to the middle of the porch.

Bessie leapt right in her way. "If you don't want to catch grasshoppers, let's push each other on the rope swing and jump off," said Bessie. "See who can jump farthest."

A burning anger rose up in Clara's chest and

heated up her face. She'd like to push Bessie, all right. She'd like to push her so hard she'd fly off the rope swing and into the creek.

"If you're so biggity, Bessie, let's see you jump over one of Momma's crocks," she said. The danger of her suggestion made a thin crack in her anger. If Momma knew what they were up to . . . She stood back from the crock, moving quickly to cover her fear.

"I'll jump over one," said Bessie, "if you'll jump two."

Clara measured herself against the crock. It came up above her knees. "I could jump two," she said, trying to make her voice sound sure. Daddy said she had long legs now that she was in her tens, just like the legs on a newborn mule. "Maybe even three. I just don't want to."

"You can't. It's too far."

"Not for me." She thought quickly. "I'll jump three if you jump two." That would shut Bessie up. She could never make it over two.

"Dare you," said Bessie.

Clara felt cornered. Bessie knew she'd never walk

away from a dare. "All right, I take your dare. But you go first."

Bessie shook her head hard, making her braids fly side to side. "It was your idea. You go first." She put her hands on her hips, looking for all the world like Momma. That finished Clara off. She was tired of being bossed around.

"Just you watch, Bessie Raglan." Clara pulled two more crocks in line with the first.

Bessie's eyes went round and scared. "I take back my dare."

"Too late," said Clara. She'd need a running start. She had to go high, and she had to go far. She crossed to the other side of the porch and pushed her father's rocking chair out of the way. She figured she just had room to land without falling into Momma's bee balm.

Clara's feet flashed. She leapt up, and the red blur of the bee balm came rushing at her. She tucked her knees higher. She'd show Bessie! But when she stretched out her legs to land, her heel struck the rounded edge of the third crock. It tipped over and hit the porch with a hollow thud. Clara fell straight down, her shoulder crashing into the splintery wood.

The chickens exploded into the air, beating their wings and screeching in alarm. As Clara watched, stunned, the crock rolled toward the edge of the porch. She grabbed for it, but she wasn't fast enough. The crock dropped onto the hard earth and broke in half like an overripe watermelon.

chapter two

"You're in trouble now," Bessie said, hopping from one foot to the other. "Momma, Momma!"

"Hush, Bessie," Clara hissed. She tried to sit up, but a sharp pain caught her side.

"Momma, Momma!" Bessie's voice got higher.

Momma pushed open the door, drying her hands on a piece of burlap sack. "Who'd I see flying by the window?"

"Clara," Bessie said. "She fell."

Momma walked over and helped Clara to sit up. "You all right, Sugarcake?"

"Yes'm," said Clara, but she felt light and trembly inside.

"What're you girls doing, anyway?"

"Jumping," Clara mumbled, getting to her feet.

"Clara broke a crock," said Bessie, still hopping up and down.

"You dared me!" Clara answered, quicklike.

"Did not, did not." Bessie's voice was squeaky. "I took my dare back."

Momma looked over to the end of the porch. "Blessed Jesus!" One hand flew up and grabbed the dime hanging around her neck.

She dropped down between the bushes and picked up the two big halves of the crock. She turned them until the edges fit together. Even from the porch, Clara could see light coming through where small pieces were missing.

When Momma looked up, she was mad—so mad she was all cold and quiet.

Shame filled Clara, and anger at her carelessness.

"Now how am I going to put up enough sausage to get us through the winter?" asked Momma. Her voice cut through Clara, cold as a winter wind. "I've got to have all four crocks." She laid the broken pieces on the porch by Clara's feet.

Clara didn't say anything. Bessie stopped hopping and stood, silent.

"Clara, you're quick as a rabbit and as thoughtless, too," said Momma.

Waves of shame ran through Clara, making a hissing sound in her ears. "I'll take the eggs to the barterman," she said. "Trade them for another crock." She would even take Blackberry's eggs, too, once she found the nest. Blackberry could lay more later for bitties.

"Hunh!" Momma's foot tapped angrily on the porch. "That all you got to say? We ain't got enough eggs for no crock, Clara. You know I trade our eggs for flour."

"But didn't you get the crock from the barterman?"

"Sure we did, right after Bessie was born. We had to decide between a crock and a wool blanket. Daddy said if we put an extra log on the fire, we could get by with our quilts. He wore himself out that fall, sawing up extra wood." Momma folded her arms across her chest. "That crock cost twenty cents a gallon." She nodded at the crock halves. "That's a ten-gallon crock you just broke."

"I know, Momma," Clara whispered. She could figure it out pretty quick. Twenty cents a gallon for a ten-gallon crock came to two dollars.

"No telling what they cost now," continued Momma. "Maybe twenty-five cents a gallon."

That would be two dollars and fifty cents. How would she ever get that much money?

"Now get out of my sight for a while," said Momma. "I'm going down in my garden alone to get that sage. I need to get ahold of myself."

"I'm sorry, Momma."

"Can't eat apologies, Clara." Momma turned on the steps. "And take Bessie with you."

Clara watched Momma walk down between the rows of hollyhocks and butterbeans. Catnip lined one side of the path, and boneset the other. When Momma got to the sage, she squatted down. With a fast, twisting motion, she broke off a long stem.

Clara wanted to call out and somehow make Momma understand that it was an accident. But the pungent smell of the sage seemed to catch in her throat, keeping her silent.

"What're we going to do?" whispered Bessie.

"Hush up," said Clara.

The day lay in pieces like the broken crock. She stood on the porch, listening to the bees. But now their buzzing had a sharp edge.

Her mind went back to the barterman. Every two weeks he came into town, his old brown-and-white horse slowly pulling a peddling wagon piled high with goods. The barterman took eggs and wild herbs and homemade butter. He traded them for factory-made goods from far away, like needles and fabric and crocks and bottles. And the barterman took sang. Most years Daddy found a little sang, maybe two or three plants, if he looked long enough and if he got lucky.

Clara ran into the house. In the corner were two big barrels that Momma kept full of water, then against the wall was a long counter for cooking and washing up. Above that, Daddy had built shelves. Momma kept everything neat as a pin. Clara knew right where to go. Under the shelf holding the tin cups and plates was a tidy stack of burlap bags. She grabbed one and ran back outside.

"Come on," she said to Bessie.

They walked past Momma and the growing pile of sage. Momma didn't even glance up. Just beyond the barn, Clara found the faint beginning of the deer trail that headed into the woods.

"Where are we going?" Bessie asked in a small voice.

"Hunting," said Clara.

chapter three

Clara had followed the deer path into the wooded hills behind their house many times before. She and Bessie even had a secret hiding spot in an old stump back there. But, except with Daddy, she'd never gone farther, never climbed Red Owl Mountain, which rose steeply behind the hills. But that's where she was going now.

She headed up the narrow path to the top of the first hill, then down the other side, then up another hill and down. Behind her she heard Bessie's feet crunching in the dry leaves. Before her stood Red Owl.

With a little gasp, Clara started up the mountain. The slope was steeper, the woods thicker and more tangled. But she could still pick out the deer path. She figured as long as they stayed on it, they'd be all right.

Sweat dampened the back of her neck as she climbed. She rubbed it with the burlap sack.

"Wait for me," Bessie whined.

Clara stopped quickly. She'd almost forgotten Bessie was with her.

All around her, the maples were turning yellow and the bee gums were going to red. A sharp gust of wind scattered leaves to the ground. It felt like a thunderstorm coming up. One of those fall storms that could be on you right quick.

"What are we looking for? Blackberry?" Bessie asked when she caught up. All the challenge had faded from her eyes.

Clara took her sister's hand and intertwined her fingers with Bessie's. She liked seeing their fingers laced together—hers a deep, warm brown, Bessie's a lighter golden brown. "We're not looking for the hen," Clara said. "She's nesting way back near the house."

"Oh," said Bessie in a small voice.

"We're after sang," Clara went on. "It's a medicine herb the barterman wants. He calls it ginseng. I'm going to trade him for a new crock for Momma."

Clara knew Bessie didn't like getting way out in the woods. She was afraid of poisonous snakes. Momma kept the bushes cut down around the house, and there was a black racer living next to the barn that drove off the rattlers and copperheads. But up here in the woods a snake could be right next to where you stepped, and you wouldn't even know till it hauled off and bit you.

Clara picked her way along, holding Bessie's hand. Far off in the woods she thought she heard whistling. A shiver went up her back. No one lived on Red Owl Mountain. Who could be out here, besides her and Bessie?

"You hear somebody whistling?" Clara asked.

Bessie's eyes opened wide. "Maybe it's haunts."

Clara glanced around, scared at the thought of

ghosts. All she saw were trees and the deer path winding back down the mountain.

"There's no haunts in the daytime, Bessie," she said, hoping she was right. "Must be mockingbirds."

Bessie didn't seem convinced. "It might be a haunt calling us, trying to get us to cross over to . . . to . . ."

The hairs on the back of Clara's neck stood up. Granny, Daddy's momma, said that when the haunts called, they were trying to get you to cross over into death with them. She took a deep breath.

"We're not going with you," she hollered. Just to be sure, she faced the other way and hollered again. That would keep a haunt from taking you.

"Now come on, Bessie."

"What does a haunt look like, anyway?" asked Bessie, slipping in the leaves.

"Mostly you can't see them. But they can take the shape of an animal."

"Any animal?"

"I suppose mostly they try to be a big animal, so nothing can get them while they're shaped like that." Clara gave her sister's hand a tug. "Now come on."

She had other things to worry about beside haunts. A month ago, she and Daddy had gone looking for sang two days in a row and had come home empty-handed. Daddy had been disappointed. Clara knew he wanted to trade the barterman for some calico Momma was wanting. What if she couldn't find any sang now?

They walked up the deer path without talking. Clara could see through the trees that they were almost to the top of Red Owl. In a sudden burst, she ran ahead to the level clearing. She peered down the far side, searching for bright red ginseng berries. She could remember exactly how they looked from last year, when Daddy had showed her a patch across the valley near Little Frog Creek.

Overhead, a dove made a liquid *too-coo* sound. Clara stood still a moment, listening for that whistling again. The air was getting thick and moist and hard to breathe.

Bessie kicked her feet in the leaves.

"Hush, Lil Bits." It made her feel better, somehow bigger, to call her sister by her nickname. Still and all, she had a funny feeling running up her back that somebody was behind them, watching.

To break her twitchy feeling, she said, "Daddy told me that up here on top of Red Owl, you're smack in the middle of Tennessee.

"South Carolina's over that way, to the east." Clara pointed. "And Georgia's way down there, south. Daddy brought me up here last year on New Year's Day, 1900. It was mighty cold. But he said it would be good luck to start the century seeing as far as I could."

Clara looked back the way they had come. Their cabin was hidden from view, but she could see a handful of houses at the bottom of the valley. Then the mountains rose steeply again on the far side.

High up on the far slope was a tiny cabin in a little clearing. The hoodoo man lived there. Every night she looked across the valley at the dark mountain and saw a pinprick of light shining from his lamp.

Clara knew that Daddy had gone up to the

hoodoo man's house when he'd moved into their valley last spring. Together the two men had plowed a patch for corn and pumpkins and runner beans with Daddy's mule, Buckshot.

But Momma hadn't let Clara go. Momma said a hoodoo man could put a hex on you real bad. If somebody wanted you dead, they got a flannel bag from the hoodoo man filled with graveyard dirt and some of your hair trimmings. Then they stuck that bag under your doorstep. That fixed you good. Unless somebody found that bag and took the hex off, you were dead, all right—cemetery dead.

Clara shivered. Above the trees, clouds were piling up, darkening the midday sky. They just had to find some sang. And it had to be soon.

She peered down the mountain, squinting her eyes in the graying light. Leaves of every shade of brown and yellow and orange covered the ground. But way down the slope, Clara saw a patch of plants with bright yellow leaves and red berry pods growing at the top. With a yelp, she ran down the slope.

"Wait for me!" yelled Bessie.

Clara kept going, sliding on the fallen leaves until

she came to a stop in front of the patch. Gently she felt the pod and looked over the leaves. Bessie thumped into her back just as Clara turned from the plant in disgust. "This ain't sang. It's Indian turnip."

"Then can we go home now?" Bessie's voice sounded thin, like a hungry barnyard cat. "You can come back another time and look for sang by yourself."

"Oh, hush up," said Clara.

"Well, it wasn't me that broke Momma's crock."

Clara didn't bother to answer. Now what should she do? Give up and go home? She hated that she'd been fooled by Indian turnip. That and five-leaf poison vine could fool just about anybody from a distance.

Far off, she heard a warning rumble of thunder, and her chest felt tight from the hot, damp air. She looked up the mountain slope. She could probably look a lot farther if she came back tomorrow without Bessie.

"All right, let's go home," she said. "Let's cut around the low side of Red Owl till we join up with the deer path." That would save them going back to the top of the mountain and down again.

Bessie gave her a scared look but didn't say anything. Clara could see her watching every step she took, looking out for snakes.

Clara skirted a flat rock, seeing in her mind where they'd join up with the path. Suddenly she stopped. There at her feet were two small plants with thin golden leaves. Clara bent down. The leaves grew off either side of the stem in threes, like a young sang plant. If they were sang plants, where had their seeds come from? Clara straightened up.

She looked all around, but couldn't see any more sang. Had someone planted the berries here? If they had come from a big plant, the berries would have rolled downhill. Slowly, Clara walked up the slope. She pushed her way through a low bramble patch, the tiny thorns scratching her legs. Behind her she could hear Bessie whimpering as she picked her way along.

Right under a huge black walnut tree, Clara spotted a cluster of plants, partly hidden by tall maidenhair ferns. Was she being fooled again by Indian turnip?

She scrambled uphill to the plants. There were large clusters of bright red berries at the top of each stalk. The long, thin leaves were turning golden yellow.

She whooped with joy. It was sang, all right. She grabbed her sister in a big bear hug.

"Sang plants! Seven or eight of them. All big and strong." She spun Bessie in a circle, making her feet fly out.

"Is it enough for a crock?" asked Bessie.

"I don't know for sure. But it's plenty to find at one time."

A blue flash of lightning lit up the sky. Moments passed, then there was a faraway rumble of thunder.

"Storm's coming," said Clara. "We better dig out these roots right quick." She searched the ground till she found a strong, short oak branch. Kneeling down, she dug around the closest plant. The earth was hard, and she didn't want to break any of the little rootlets growing off the sides.

Bessie stood nearby, talking while Clara dug. "Why does the barterman want this sang?"

"I don't know." With her fingertips Clara felt the root lying sideways under the surface. Carefully she pushed the loosened dirt away. "Daddy says they send it halfway round the world to China." She had looked at a map of China in the geography book at school. It was a huge country full of long mountain ranges and rushing rivers with names like Yangtze and Si Kiang.

"Why do they send it to China?"

Clara shrugged. "They boil it up into a medicine tea. Mighty bitter, I expect." Once when Daddy was sick he'd taken a big swallow of bitters made with sang and other herbs. He'd screwed his face up and practically spit the whole mouthful out. "That'd cure a mule," he'd said.

"Why don't they dig their own?"

Clara hunched over, rocking her stick back and forth under the root. It was at least as long as her hand, and as fat as two fingers. "Maybe they liked it so much, they dug it all up." That was hard to imagine, in a country so large.

Bessie peered over Clara's shoulder. "What do you think that root will fetch from the barterman?"

"Hush, Bessie. You ask too many questions." She eased the root out and started in on the next one.

Clara tried to remember when Daddy took sang to the barterman last year. How many roots had he traded for that little keg of nails? Was a crock worth more sang than nails, or less?

Bessie interrupted her thoughts. "What have you got in that sack?"

"It's empty, Lil Bits," she answered impatiently, without looking up. "It's for the sang."

But another voice answered as well—a deep, gravelly voice. "I've got all kinds of plants in there."

Clara stood up fast and spun around.

The man in front of her wore old patchy overalls and carried a bulging tow sack. She had seen him only once before, in summer, when she and Bessie and Momma had walked into town with eggs and fresh blackberries for the barterman. There he was, the hoodoo man, standing next to the barterman's wagon.

Quick as anything, Momma had turned them right

around. They had run back to where Daddy was working with Buckshot. After Momma explained, Daddy took the eggs and blackberries down to the barterman. Momma hurried Bessie and Clara back to the house.

And now here was Bessie talking to the hoodoo man, natural as could be.

chapter four

The hoodoo man was old, but he stood tall. His skin was a rich mahogany red, all creased and weathered. His eyes were sharp and clear.

He put Clara in mind of the time last spring when she went down to close the henhouse at dusk. Next to the open door was a fox, rusty red all over with a white tip on its tail. That fox should have turned and run, but he didn't. He twitched his ears forward and stared at her with golden brown eyes. They seemed to look right down inside her. She was the one who had turned and run.

Without thinking, Clara reached out and grabbed for Bessie with one hand. With the other, she clutched the sang plant tight to her chest. She could feel her heart racketing around, making the leaves quiver. Her mind was swirling. How could he have snuck up on her? He's the hoodoo man, she answered herself. That's how.

"I'm Old Sugar Johnson," he said.

Clara knew she should say, "Pleased to meet you, Mr. Johnson." But she couldn't seem to get those proper words out of her mouth. "You're the hoodoo man," she blurted out instead.

"That's what the lovesick say," he agreed, "coming to me, asking me to make up a little red flannel bag. It fixes their loved one to them forevermore. No harm done."

Momma sure didn't think that way.

Clara's eyes flickered from the hoodoo man to the sang plants still in the ground. She wanted to pull Bessie's hand, run all the way home, and slam the door shut. But she didn't want to leave the sang for the hoodoo man. It was hers.

Clara wriggled her toes into the dirt. Momma always said she was too stubborn for her own good.

"I'm Clara," she said, finally finding her manners. "George and Lucille Raglan's daughter."

The hoodoo man nodded. "I'm acquainted with your daddy."

"This here is Bessie," said Clara.

"How do," said the hoodoo man, sweeping off an imaginary hat and bowing.

Bessie giggled. Clara yanked on her hand and gave her a warning glance. A sharp gust of wind sent leaves swirling.

Clara wondered why the hoodoo man was way out here on Red Owl Mountain with a storm coming up.

"I was fetching some plants," he said, as if he knew what Clara was thinking. "There's a lot of food and medicine herbs out here in these woods. You just got to ramble round and find them."

Clara knew. Granny said the wild curing herbs were stronger than the poor peakedy ones you could grow in your garden.

"I see y'all got a good patch of sang," the hoodoo man went on. He swung his tow sack off his back, holding it by the coarse string threaded through the top. "You want help digging it?"

"No!" said Clara. Her voice seemed too sharp and loud in the stillness of the woods. He might think if he helped dig, he could have some of it. And she needed it, more than he could possibly know. "Thank you anyway. I can get it myself," she said more quietly. She laid her root gently on the ground.

Pulling Bessie with her, she squatted down beside the sang patch. Her hands were shaking as she shoved her stick under a root and began twisting. Easy, she reminded herself. Take it easy. Otherwise you're going to bust up this here root, and it won't be any good. Bessie sat down cross-legged and started digging the dirt with her fingernails.

Old Sugar picked up Clara's root. "This must be six, seven years old, just big enough to dig." Clara didn't need a hoodoo man to tell her that. Once, she and Daddy had found a patch that he said was only three or four years old, and they had left it. Trouble was, when they came back the next year, someone else had already found it and taken the sang.

Clara glanced at the hoodoo man but kept digging. She wished he'd put her root down. Lightning flashed again. This time the thunder was closer. She gave a last twist with her stick and eased out a second root. Quickly, she started on the next.

"Your Momma might not like you girls out in this weather."

Bessie looked up at the sky, then went back to helping Clara with her fingernails.

Clara could hear the wind lashing the treetops, setting them swaying and groaning. But no hoodoo man was going to tell her what to do.

"I got time," she said.

"Not much," he replied. "This storm is going to be on us right quick. But suit yourself."

The air was so thick now, it reminded her of wash days when the house was all hot and steamy from the big, boiling tubs of water and clothes. Clara wished it would start raining so she could breathe.

"I like to work my own remedy," Old Sugar said. He sat down next to Bessie and tossed Clara's root onto the ground. The coming storm didn't seem to make no never-mind to him. "If you get sores, you gather up Saint-John's from out in the field. Then you get the little bumps growing on a gum tree. You burn them together and tie them on that sore. It'll heal right up."

Clara wondered what else he knew how to make. Poisons, if Momma was right.

"Look at this," said Old Sugar. He turned his tow sack upside down and emptied its contents onto the ground. "This here is bark off the wild cherry tree. It's called lung balm. You can boil it up into a medicine tea for coughing."

He scooped up a handful of small, brown nuts. "And the wild hickory nuts are ripe and dropping off the trees right now." He separated out nine or ten dark, bumpy roots. "These here are pig potatoes."

Clara couldn't help looking over. "Our granny makes those into a pudding," she said.

Old Sugar nodded. "I like them roasted in the ashes, or fried in lard with brown sugar." He pulled at a clump of leafy plants. "I found rabbit tobacco and church steeples. And here's some yarrow. You can make it into a poultice to stop bleeding. God put all these plants here for us to use. We just need to figure out how."

A big, cold raindrop hit the back of Clara's head. Five more sang plants in the ground. She didn't want to leave them for the hoodoo man, but right now she better get Bessie home. She shoved her stick in hard and wrenched the sang plant out of the ground. The tip of the root busted off.

"You can come back for the rest another time," said Old Sugar. "I won't touch it."

Clara felt her face get hot. It seemed as if he knew what she was thinking. Again. She pulled the red berries off the top of the plants she'd dug up and scattered them across the leaves. Daddy was mighty particular about laying the seeds back down so they could grow again.

"Y'all carry a bit of devil's shoestring in your pocket?" Old Sugar asked. "You should. It will keep the snakes from biting you." He reached in the pocket of his overalls and brought out a dried root. It was long as his hand and thin. He broke off half and offered it to Clara.

"I ain't afraid of snakes," Clara said. It wasn't exactly true, but if the hoodoo man knew how many things she was afraid of he'd probably laugh himself into tomorrow.

"Suit yourself," he said with a shrug. But Bessie reached out. The hoodoo man dropped the devil's shoestring in her hand, and she shoved it into her pocket.

"See them little roots coming off the sides of that sang?" said Old Sugar. "Now, if you get a stomach colic, you chew up some of them and swallow the juice. It'll burn as it goes down, but in a few minutes you'll feel fine."

"How come you know all about herbs?" Clara asked, though another raindrop fell on her arm.

"My Auntie Charlotte Rose was a root doctor. I took sick when I was about your age. I was powerful sick, just burning up with fever. That was back in slavery times, and we didn't have doctors. Auntie Charlotte Rose took care of me by working the roots."

Clara looked around, wondering what medicines he saw nearby. She knew a few of the plant cures, and so did Momma. And Nell—her friend Annie Mae's momma—was a midwife, and she knew a lot more. Root medicine, Nell called it.

"Master sold my momma when I was just a baby and gave me to Auntie Charlotte Rose to raise up," said the hoodoo man. "She worked in Missus' kitchen. I remember sitting on her knee while she churned butter, and hanging on to her apron while she was cooking. But when the washing-up was done, she used to go around to all the slave cabins, taking care of people with her root medicine. On Sunday afternoons, she'd take me out in the hills collecting wild plants.

"After the War between the States, when freedom came, they turned us loose just like cattle." Anger edged his words. "No land to farm, no mules, nothing. We went into the hills. We made do, catching possum, squirrel, raccoons. Auntie Charlotte Rose knew what plants to eat. And she kept seeing to everybody with her root medicine."

Rain was falling in big, cold drops, pulling Clara out of the hoodoo man's story. She wanted to hear more. But maybe that was how hoodoo worked. After he got your trust—Swoosh!—he put a fix on you. She shoved her roots into the burlap sack. "C'mon, Lil Bits. Time to light out."

As they headed back toward the deer path, Clara couldn't shake that prickly feeling on the back of her neck—as if the fox was keeping an eye on her.

They walked quickly through the hard rain for a few minutes. Then Clara said, "Bessie, I reckon we'd better not tell Momma who we been talking to."

"You telling me to lie?" asked Bessie.

"No," said Clara. "Just don't tell. That ain't lying."

chapter five

The rain was falling in sheets when they finally reached the top of the hill behind their house. Clara held the burlap sack tight to her chest, hoping to keep the sang dry. She took big, gulping breaths of the fresh, clear air.

Down below her, she could see Momma's herb and flower garden, a smudge of purples and pinks and greens. On one side of the garden were the barn and the pigpen. Past that was the outhouse, a little dark patch in the rain. On the other side of the garden stood their one-room cabin, edged by the bee balm. Smoke was struggling up from the chimney.

Lightning snaked down from the clouds, striking the far hills across the valley.

"Come on, Bessie, Momma's got a fire going." Wind whipped the rain every which way, making Clara feel cold to her bones. A crash of thunder cut through Bessie's reply.

"This is a real frog-strangler!" hollered Clara. Even the rain and lightning and cold couldn't take away her excited feeling about gathering the sang. But she could see Bessie was shivering. Maybe if they ran, Bessie would warm up.

"Race you home," Clara hollered. Without waiting, she took off down the slope, sliding and skidding on the wet leaves till she hit flat ground. Ducking her head, she ran alongside the barn, mud squishing up between her toes. She sped past Momma's garden, then she was on the porch.

"Gracious!" said Momma as Clara ran into the house. "You look like a drowned cat." Momma was at the table, smoothing flat an empty flour sack that she was making into underclothes.

Hanging on the rafters above Bessie and Clara's bed was the sage Momma had collected. The sweetness of the sage mixed with a warm, meaty smell coming from the iron pot on the fire. They were having the possum Daddy shot yesterday. Clara's mouth watered. She hadn't eaten since breakfast.

"Look what I got." She held up the burlap sack, swinging it above her head. "Sang! We can trade it to the barterman for a crock."

"Takes a lot of sang to get a crock." Momma's dime gleamed. "Where's Lil Bits?"

"She's right behind me," said Clara. "Just look at this sang." She opened the sack wide and watched Momma carefully to see if she was still angry. "And there are four more roots up on Red Owl Mountain."

Momma peered into the bag. "You got some nice roots in there. Just be careful and don't shake any dirt on my clean flour sack."

"Yes'm."

Momma picked up her big scissors and started cutting the soft cotton. She didn't seem angry.

"Who's that for?"

"Lil Bits. You had the last one."

Clara's had been covered with little yellow and white daisies. This one was printed with rows of pink rosebuds. Clara liked the roses better.

"And mind the mending," Momma said.

"Yes'm."

Beside Momma's elbow was a stack of mending from some white folks in town. On top was a pale yellow nightgown with lace and a pink ribbon. Clara was wishing she could touch it when Bessie burst in, wet and mad. Her thin cotton dress was sticking to her. "You took a head start," she said, slamming the door behind her.

"Did not."

"Did."

"What's the matter with you girls?" Momma grabbed a rag and dried Bessie's hair with it. "Go stand in front of the fire, Lil Bits. You're soaking wet."

Clara squeezed next to Bessie in front of the fire. Wind blew in through the walls where chinking had fallen out, pushing cold gusts of air into the cabin.

"Clara, just look how cold Lil Bits is." Momma touched Bessie's forehead. "You should have brought her back earlier, you hear?"

"Yes, ma'am." Wasn't it just like Momma to make it her fault that the storm had caught them? Clara climbed up on Momma's rocking chair, balancing carefully. She hung the sack over a rafter near the fireplace, far away from Momma's mending. The sooner the sang dried, the sooner she could trade it to the barterman.

Other bags hung from the rafters, full of dried apples, huckleberries, and blackberries. In the winter, Momma would soak some of the fruit in water. She'd mix up lard with the soft, white flour she got from the peddling wagon and make a crust. Then she'd cook up two half-moon pies in the frying pan. Clara especially loved the first bite, when the crust would break under her teeth and the sweet, tart berries would fill her mouth.

She jumped down off the rocking chair, her stomach tightening with hunger.

"How'd you find so much sang?" asked Momma,

tucking sweet potatoes into the coals. "That's the first I heard of any being found this year."

Clara shrugged. "Just kept looking."

"I saw it first," said Bessie.

"I dug it up," said Clara.

"Good for colic, too," said Bessie.

"That's right, Lil Bits," said Momma. "How'd you know that?"

Clara shot a warning glance at Bessie, but Bessie wasn't looking.

"The hoodoo man said."

"Bessie!" cried Clara.

Momma's hand flew up to the silver dime. "Is that true?" she asked Clara.

Clara studied the floor.

"Three weeks' shame on you, Clara, for not telling me. Now look at me when I'm speaking to you."

Clara looked up.

"You seen the hoodoo man?"

"Yes'm."

"For how long?"

"Not long, Momma. Honest."

"Clara, you better just sit down right now and tell me what happened."

"Ain't nothing to tell," said Clara, staying on her feet. "When we were looking for sang, he happened along and talked with us. Then he left. That's all."

"He didn't get ahold of anything of yours, did he? Or Bessie's?"

"No, ma'am." Clara felt her ears get hot with all the angry words she was holding inside her. Momma had no idea what it was like, always minding Bessie, always getting blamed for every last skinny little thing.

"It wasn't my fault the hoodoo man found us, Momma."

Momma grabbed Clara by the shoulders. "You're the hardest child to understand." Momma gave her a tight little shake. "Why do you think I wear this dime? To keep hoodoo away, that's why."

Streaks of fear ran down Clara's back. "You said it was for headaches." Why hadn't Momma told her the truth about the dime a long time ago? Momma keeping it a secret made it more frightening.

"Daddy didn't want me scaring you girls." Momma

gave a short laugh. "But you can get a fix put on you anytime, Clara. Anytime. You got to be careful."

"How does the dime keep hoodoo away?"

"Anybody tries to put a fix on us, the dime will tarnish, turn dark gray."

Momma peered at the dime. "Still bright. Now listen to me, Clara. There's plenty of good reason to stay away from the hoodoo man."

"What reason, Momma?"

"Ain't for children to know."

chapter six

Outside a mule brayed.

"There's your daddy now, coming home from Mr. King's place with Buckshot."

Clara went out to the porch. The rain had turned to a light mist. Daddy and Buckshot were walking up through the field. A patch of sunlight broke through the clouds, shining right on them. Clara thought they looked just like a picture out of the preacher's Bible.

She ran down to meet them. She wanted to see Daddy before Momma told him how she broke the crock and talked to the hoodoo man and let Bessie get wet and cold.

"Guess what I have," Daddy said.

"Peppermint candies?" They were Clara's favorite, and she didn't get them more than once or twice a year.

Clara put one hand on Buckshot's harness, right on the smooth leather patch Daddy had sewn, and fell into step with them.

"Now where would I get peppermints?" he asked. "Guess again."

"Tell," she begged.

Daddy reached down into his shirt and brought out a half-grown wild rabbit. "I found him nesting in Mr. King's barn when I moved a saddle."

"He's not for eating, is he?" Clara held her breath. The rabbit was a soft grayish brown, with big ears and a white tail. He blinked fearfully at her.

"No," said Daddy. "He's too little. You and Bessie can play with him for a while, then we'll let him go at dusk. Mr. King won't want him back in his barn, chewing on everything. The rabbit will find a new nest out in the fields around here."

Clara took the rabbit, holding him tight. He kicked hard with his back feet.

"Cover his head so he feels safe," said Daddy.

Quickly she tucked him under her chin, covering his head with her hand. She could feel him snuggling in, butting his forehead and making digging motions with his paws.

"He scratches!"

The rabbit gave a final push with his nose and then lay pressed tight against her neck. She could feel a quivering running through him.

"Thinks he's in his nest, doesn't he?" Daddy smiled. "Why don't you take him into the house and show Lil Bits."

Clara held the rabbit a moment longer. She knew the minute Daddy set eyes on Momma, he'd want to know what was upsetting her. Clara sure didn't want to be around when Momma told him. She handed the rabbit carefully back to Daddy. "You show Bessie. I'll put Buckshot away."

Daddy looked surprised, but he didn't say anything. He handed her his sack full of tools for leather work. Inside were things like a knife and a hole punch and long thick needles—some curved, some straight—and heavy black thread. He even had a round chunk of beeswax, for smoothing the thread, and a piece of leather hide he threw over his legs so he wouldn't hurt himself while he worked. Folks said their harnesses and saddles were twice as good as new when Daddy was done.

Clara slung the sack over her shoulder and led Buckshot to the barn. The henhouse next to the barn was empty, the chickens nowhere to be seen. Out ranging around, Clara thought, scratching through the wet fallen leaves for bugs and tender plants.

Clara was careful to keep her gaze away from the pigpen. She couldn't bear to look in that hog's face when it was getting close to butchering time. It seemed like he might see his future in her eyes, and who'd want to know a thing like that?

At butchering time, all the neighbors would come over to help. There'd be men shouting and the hog screaming. While Daddy was cutting up the meat, Momma would build a fire under the pig pot and throw big hunks of fat in.

Last year Momma made Clara stand over the pig pot for hours, stirring the fat as it melted down into lard. The smoke kept after her, stinging her eyes and filling her throat.

Clara put her hand to her stomach. It made her feel sick just thinking about it. This year she was going to run down to Annie Mae's house when the butchering started, just see if she didn't.

Inside the barn she brushed out Buckshot's damp coat, feeling his breathing as she worked over his broad chest and shoulders. He smelled good, like rain and dirt and grass all mixed together. Daddy had bought Buckshot before Clara was born for five dollars from the Dawsons. They bred the best mules for miles around. They let Buckshot go cheap because he used to jump straight up in the air whenever he was startled. When he came down, he ran without thinking. "Takes off like a shot," Mr. Dawson said. Daddy told her it took the better part of a year to get Buckshot calmed down.

Buckshot blew impatiently into her hair. With a start, Clara realized she had stopped brushing. If only she knew what Momma was saying to Daddy right now. She swung an arm up and rubbed his large head. "It's all right, Buckshot," she murmured, knowing she meant, "Hope I'm all right."

Finally, Buckshot was brushed out. Clara even combed the tangles from his mane and tail, and gave him fresh water and an armful of sweet hay. She couldn't put it off any longer. Time to go inside.

The chickens were gathering in front of the hen-house, moving toward the safety of home as the day ended. Soon as it was dusk, they'd go inside and hop up on the old broom handle that was their roost. She noticed with relief that Blackberry was with them. Still not broody. She'd have another chance to follow her.

Bessie popped out onto the porch. "Suppertime," she hollered.

"I'm coming," Clara called.

Everyone was sitting at the table when she walked in. Quickly, she slid into her seat. While Daddy said grace, she took deep breaths of the warm, meaty smell. It felt like her front and back were rubbing together with hunger. She looked quickly from Momma to Daddy. He knew, she could tell. But Momma didn't look mad. Somehow that squeezed-up place in Momma always softened when Daddy was home. Maybe things would go better now.

"Where's the rabbit?" Clara asked Bessie, as Momma served up the stewed possum and sweet potatoes.

"Momma put him in a basket with a dish towel over the top."

Clara looked around.

"He's under my chair," Bessie whispered.

As soon as she finished eating, Clara asked Daddy, "You going to tell a story tonight?" She was looking forward to holding the rabbit while he talked.

Daddy raised his eyebrows. "I will after Momma and I set out the pig pot. We'll be needing it soon."

Clara jumped to her feet. "I'll help you get it, Daddy. I'm strong enough."

"I believe you are, Sugarcake." He pushed back his chair. "All right, let's go."

"Let's get the supper dishes cleaned up, Bessie," said Momma. "Then I'll start sewing your underclothes." Momma set the kerosene lamp on the table and lit the wick with a flaming twig from the fireplace.

Clara walked alongside Daddy through the dusky light. Maybe Momma hadn't told him about the sang she had found. All by herself. She was about to say something when Daddy said, "Better close the chickens in now, Clara."

She ran over to the henhouse and slipped inside the low door. The chickens were up on their roost, side by side, their heads drawn down, eyes closed. Clara knew they weren't asleep yet, because they were still talking to one another. *"Brrr, brrr,"* they muttered back and forth, shifting their feet on the old broom handle. She found Blackberry wedged in between two small brown hens. She reached over and gave her a gentle stroke.

Blackberry opened one eye and looked straight at Clara. *"Brrr,"* she said, deep in her throat.

Clara laughed gently. "Tomorrow," she whispered, "I'm finding your nest."

Backing out, she latched the henhouse door and then slipped into the barn. Buckshot stamped his feet and let out his breath in greeting. Clara reached up and touched the velvety softness of his nose as she passed his stall.

Daddy was far back in the shadowy darkness, moving hoes, pitchforks, and shovels. "The pig pot's behind here," he said.

"Daddy," she began.

He handed her a bridle. "Set that over on the peg by the door, Clara."

She held it tight, feeling the metal bite into her hand. "I found sang today," she said. Her voice was quiet but proud. "A whole patch. Up on Red Owl Mountain."

Daddy stopped shifting tools. "Momma said you also found the hoodoo man."

She felt something fall from her stomach to her feet. Like the time she saw a tiny green humming-bird fly into a windowpane and drop, lifeless, to the ground. "He found us, Daddy. We didn't find him." Momma must have made it sound like Clara went looking for that old hoodoo man.

"Why is Momma so scared of him, anyway?"

Daddy just shook his head and leaned on a hoe. It seemed like he was standing in disappointment. "Clara, you cause your mother no end of worry," he said softly.

"Yes, sir," Clara said quickly, because she didn't want him to say anything more. Maybe she'd never make Daddy proud of her again. Maybe she'd never know why Momma was scared of the hoodoo man. She spun on her heel and carried the bridle over to the nail.

"I've got the pot," Daddy said. Hearing that, Clara knew he wouldn't say anything more about being disappointed. She pushed past the tools and stood next to the pot. It nearly came up to her hips and was bigger around than Daddy's shoulders.

Daddy stuck a strong pole under the rounded handle. "Get your shoulder under that end."

Clara bent down and eased the pole onto her shoulder. She stood up as Daddy picked up his end. The heavy pot hung between them. Clara staggered for a moment under the weight.

"Good," he said. "We'll just walk real slow, step

by step, back to the field in front of the house."

Once they got outside, it was a little easier to move, but the iron pot swayed with each step they took. It bumped roughly against Clara's legs. Her breath started coming in raggedy puffs.

"Are you all right? If it's too heavy, I'll get Momma to help."

"No," gasped Clara. She shifted the pole to a different spot on her shoulder. At least she could do this right.

Finally they made it to the field. Daddy went to the barn and came back with three old bricks and a big piece of oil cloth. He laid the bricks on the ground in a C shape and heaved the pot on top of them. Then he shook out the heavy oil cloth and laid it over the pot. "This'll keep the rain off for a few days. Tomorrow morning I'm going down to Hickory Flat. I've got four, five folks waiting for me."

Clara nodded. Daddy had grown up near Hickory Flat, and folks there saved up their leather work for him, making do till he would come by and work quietly in their barns. Granny still lived there, and four of his sisters.

They walked back to the porch. Daddy sat down in his rocking chair, and Clara sat next to him.

"Storytime," he called.

Down by the creek, the last of the sunlight seemed to catch in the willows, making the leaves blaze gold. Usually the shiny light filled Clara with joy. But tonight all the wrongness of the day was pressing in on her, making her feel gray and empty.

Daddy pulled out his pocketknife and took a piece of cedarwood from behind the rocker. He ran the knife down the length of the split wood. A paper-thin strip curled away and spun to the floor. Clara knew he'd sit whittling for a few minutes, turning over story ideas in his mind.

On a sudden impulse she ran inside and got the cigar box from under her bed. Sitting cross-legged next to Daddy, she opened the wooden lid. On top were dried violets from Annie Mae. Clara pushed them aside and lifted out one of the candle stubs she used for going to the outhouse at night. She sniffed its soft, beeswax smell. There was also a rattlesnake rattle, with seven rattles on it, and the tiny skull of a mouse, with all its teeth. In a little envelope she had three sticks of sealing wax—silver, red, and blue—that she won at the school spelling bee last year. She had never used them, because she never sent letters that would need sealing. But someday she might. Clara picked up a pink-and-tan seashell from the Gulf of Mexico and held it to her ear, listening to the soft murmur of the ocean inside.

Tucked into a corner of the box was a small bone-handled knife that Granny had given her when Clara was seven. She took it out and flipped the steel blade open with her thumbnail. "You'll know when you're going to need it," Granny had said. "It'll call out to you." Clara snapped the blade shut. Granny was always saying things that were puzzling.

Bessie pushed the door open and came out onto the porch. She was holding her dress up by the hem with the rabbit inside. Clara quickly shut the lid to her cigar box and put it behind her.

Bessie sat down cross-legged next to Clara. Daddy was whistling softly, making cedar strips curl to the floor.

Clara thought he looked like Granny from the side. But he sure was quiet compared to his momma. She'd come visiting from Hickory Flat every year, riding her old mule, Big Red. She came on the Greyland Road, riding hard for ten or twelve hours, arriving long after the stars were out. She always came on June nineteenth, to celebrate the end of slavery times. She was tall as Daddy and moved fast as lightning and smoked a corncob pipe. She loved sitting on the porch and speaking her mind.

"You know," she said at the end of every evening, "we were freed on January first, 1863, by Mr. Lincoln's proclamation." She'd wave her pipe, poking at the air around her. "But nobody told us down in Georgia! We didn't hear about it till June 'teenth."

Then she'd turn to Daddy. "And weren't you born into freedom not more than three days later? The last of my eleven children, and the first free man. Glory, glory! Mr. Lincoln is sitting on the right hand of God, if you ask me."

One morning when they woke up, she'd be gone. Clara was always sorry when she left, but she could tell Momma was relieved. Momma said Granny had Jesus and Abraham Lincoln mixed up in her mind, which didn't sit right with her.

"Time to let that rabbit go," said Daddy.

"Can't we keep him until tomorrow, Daddy?" asked Clara. She'd barely seen him. Besides, the night was full of snakes and foxes and owls, out hunting for food. "He could sleep in the basket tonight." Inside, where it was safe.

"What did I tell you? Evening is rabbit time," said Daddy.

Momma came out and sat on the top step, humming to herself. Clara loved to see Momma this way, her hands quiet and still, her eyes soft as they gazed far off above the trees.

"What are you thinking about, Momma?" Clara asked softly.

"Just talking with God, Sugarcake, talking with God."

"I want the rabbit to hear your story, Daddy," said Bessie. She peered into her skirt at the rabbit.

"He's got sharp ears," said Daddy. "He can listen from the bushes."

"Let me hold him one more time," said Clara. She squeezed next to Bessie and reached for the rabbit.

Bessie drew her knees up. "Not yet," she said.

Clara pushed past Bessie's elbow. It was her turn, and Bessie knew it. Her fingers closed around the soft fur on the rabbit's back.

With a bound, the rabbit leapt out of Clara's grasp and bolted off the porch. He ran in sudden bursts, twisting first one way and then the other through the field. He gave a final, wild jump, and Clara saw the white of his tail as he disappeared into the bushes.

Watching him, she thought of her mother's words. He was quick, all right, but not thoughtless. Just scared.

"Clara let him go," Bessie wailed next to her.

Clara sprang to her feet. "It wasn't my fault," she said.

"Nobody's blaming you, Clara," said Momma.

"Bessie is."

"Come here, Lil Bits," said Momma.

Bessie hollered louder.

"I said come here, Bessie." Momma's voice was sharp. "That rabbit is long gone."

Momma leaned over and pulled Bessie to her. She wiped Bessie's teary face and looked surprised.

"You're hot, Lil Bits. You feel sick?"

"My throat hurts." Bessie laid her head against Momma's chest and closed her eyes.

"Getting close to bedtime," said Daddy. "I better tell my story quick." He held his hands still for a moment, thinking.

"Did I ever tell you about the time our old hog, Miss Josephina, got out?"

"Lots of times, Daddy." Clara wrapped her arms tight around her legs. Daddy had a pack of stories about that hog he had when he was coming up. Usually they were about some crazy thing Miss Josephina did when she broke out of her pen. Clara always figured some of those stories were made up. No one hog could be that much trouble. But Daddy and Granny swore every story was true.

"Well," said Daddy as his knife slid down the cedarwood, "one fall day, must've been a lot like this one, Miss Josephina got out of the pen. My daddy told me to go and find her.

"I knew right where that hog was heading. Way back of our place was a big oak tree. Nothing a hog likes so much as acorns. So I hightailed it out there. Sure enough, she was running her snout all over the ground, chewing acorns as fast as she could. I was just sneaking up on her when she ran smack into a bush.

"Now, do you know what came shooting straight out that bush? A big buck rabbit, just like a hound had scared him. He took three long bounds across the grass and then stopped and turned around. I never saw a rabbit stop running before. I'll be blessed if that rabbit didn't bound back and stand in front of Miss Josephina. That hog quit rooting around and stared at that rabbit like her eyes were gonna fall right out of her head."

"Then what, Daddy?" Clara asked.

"Quick as anything, the rabbit spun around and kicked Miss Josephina right in the snout with both back feet. You should have seen her face. I never seen a hog more surprised in all my born days."

"What'd she do, Daddy?" Bessie asked from Momma's lap.

"She ran back to her pen on her short, little old legs so fast that I couldn't keep up. I don't think she tried to break out for weeks after that." Daddy stood up and brushed the long curls of cedarwood off his lap.

"Stepped on a pin,

pin bent.

That's the way

the story went," he said.

Momma was laughing. "Glad we don't own that hog," she said.

Watching Momma laugh made Clara want to catch her up in a big hug and tell her she was sorry she had caused her so much trouble and worry.

Then Momma said, "Soon we'll have enough cedar shavings to stuff a new mattress for the girls." Holding Bessie, she got to her feet. "Don't forget to close the shutters, Clara," she said as she went into the house.

The moment was gone.

Over the field, the last few fireflies of the season were circling. Clara watched as darkness settled into the spaces between the trees where gold light had been shining. After Bessie went to bed, Clara liked to sit on the porch awhile with Momma and Daddy, watching night fall. It reminded Clara of Blackberry when she had little bittie chicks. She'd settle down on the nest and tent her wings out, gently calling *tuck-tuck-tuck* to her bitties. They'd come scrambling, ducking under her wings and wriggling into the soft, downy feathers on her breast. Next moment they'd all be asleep, feeling completely safe from the foxes and weasels out in the dark.

Across the valley Clara saw the hoodoo man's light wink on. Her own safe feeling broke, and the night seemed full of hidden dangers again. Somewhere beyond the field, the little rabbit was alone, away from his hiding places in Mr. King's barn. And somewhere in that darkness were haunts.

Tiredness poured down from Clara's head to her feet. She pulled the heavy wooden shutters across the porch windows and went inside.

Momma and Bessie were kneeling next to the little bed, finishing their prayers. Momma had set the kerosene lamp on the dresser between the two beds. Seeing Bessie and Momma in the pool of lamplight made Clara ache. It seemed like she was always on the outside.

She pulled off her dress and hung it next to Bessie's on a nail over the bed. She slipped into her nightgown, mumbled her prayers, and slid into bed. Her sister felt mighty hot.

Momma blew out the light and went back on the porch with Daddy. Clara moved away from Bessie and lay still, wanting to feel the cool darkness. She could hear the murmur of her parents' voices. She couldn't quite make out the words, but then Daddy said clearly, "He ain't nothing to be afraid of."

She thought she heard Momma reply, "I just don't trust no two-shadow man."

chapter seven

Clara came awake with a start. Daddy was gently shaking her. "Bye, Sugarcake. I'll see you in a few days."

"Bye," she whispered. She tried to smile, but she didn't want him to go.

From her bed she could hear Daddy saying good-bye to Momma. For a minute their voices seemed to tangle up in her dreams, and then she was back asleep.

When Clara woke up again, Daddy was gone and Momma was cutting out biscuits at the table with an old snuff tin. The sweet, pungent smell of sage drifted down from the rafters. Clara looked up and saw her bag of sang. In the clear morning light it hung limp, looking half-empty. She threw back the blankets. She had to get up on Red Owl Mountain and collect the rest of the sang. She wanted that bag full-looking, holding out the promise of another crock.

Bessie whimpered and pulled the covers over herself.

"Good morning, Sugarcake," said Momma, pressing the biscuit cutter quickly into the dough. "After you get your chores done this morning, we'll chink the walls where the mud has fallen out."

Clara pulled her dress over her head, muffling Momma's voice. When Daddy was gone, Momma's voice took on a brittle cheerfulness. Somehow it always made Clara feel tighter inside.

Clara shook Bessie. "Get up, sleepyhead."

Bessie twisted sharply away. "Leave be," she muttered.

"Quit fussing, Lil Bits," Clara said. She peered more closely at her sister. Bessie was breathing quickly in and out. There were dark smudges under her eyes.

"Momma," Clara called softly. "I think Bessie's still sick." She stepped back from the bed. Momma was gonna blame her, sure as gravy.

Momma hurried over, dusting the flour off her hands. She put her forearm to Bessie's cheek.

"Going to be a quiet day for you, Lil Bits," said Momma.

"I'm fine," said Bessie. She kicked the blanket away and stood up. Momma caught her as she swayed sideways.

"Come over to my rocking chair, Lil Bits. Looks like Clara's going to have to do your chores this morning."

"Guess I'll get down to the barn," said Clara. She could see Momma setting her lips tight together.

"Clara." Momma's voice was firm. "You see what getting wet and cold can do to Bessie?"

"Yes'm." Clara walked backward toward the door. She was tired of having Momma fuss at her. Five steps, six. She'd be out the door in a few more steps.

"You need to be more careful next time."

"Yes'm." Clara turned and ran out the door to the barn. She wanted to get her chores done fast, then go get the rest of the sang. She sure didn't want to spend the morning here, with Bessie sick and Momma's worry hanging over everything like thick smoke.

When she was done taking care of the chickens and the hog, she cleaned out Buckshot's stall and led him to the field.

She grabbed a handful of his mane and pulled herself up on his back. He shook the flies away from his eyes and started into an easy walk down toward the stream. It felt good to be riding on his wide, steady back. Clara leaned forward and scratched Buckshot behind his ear, right where he liked it. The mule swiveled his big ears forward and back and gave a soft snort of pleasure. She rode him across the creek and tied him to a big walnut tree where he could pull up the last of the grass with his strong teeth.

"At least you ain't worried about anything," she said before she went back to the henhouse.

She only found three eggs in the nests. Now that the days were shorter, the hens weren't laying as much. Clara brought the eggs in and set them on the table next to Momma, who was stitching up Bessie's underwear. Her needle glinted as it flew in and out of the cotton. One thing about Momma, she was mighty fast with sewing. Clara didn't think she'd ever be like that.

"Biscuits waiting for you, Clara." Clara let her breath out softly. So Momma wasn't staying mad.

Bessie was rocking, her foot pushing at the floor, sending the rocking chair back and forth like a tree in a high wind. She was staring at the fire, her eyes bright. Just looking at her made Clara feel jumpy.

"Momma, I'd like to go get the rest of the sang with Annie Mae."

Momma nodded. "I think the chinking will have to wait till Bessie is better."

Clara grabbed a burlap sack and slipped two biscuits into her pockets—one for her and one for Annie Mae. She trotted through the field, followed the creek, and then took the path. Annie Mae's house was about twenty minutes down the mountain.

The sun was just clearing the treetops, taking the night chill out of the air. Clara could see how things were going to work out. She'd collect the rest of the sang and hang it up in the rafters where it would dry. Then they would take it to the barterman. Clara gave a hop of joy, imagining Momma's face when she came home with a shiny new crock. Maybe she'd have enough sang to get a few peppermint candies. Her mouth watered, thinking of the sweet, minty taste. She'd even give one to Bessie, without Momma asking.

As she walked she noticed a persimmon tree off in the distance. Clara drew in a deep breath. Hundreds of the deep orange fruits bowed down its limbs. Now, that was another good thing about the killing frost. Soon as those persimmons got frostbit, they'd be nice and soft and sweet. She'd have to show Momma the tree. Momma would make up persimmon bread and pudding. Maybe she and Momma could even make persimmon marmalade and take it to the barterman to trade.

Clara came to a sudden stop. When would the barterman come again? Annie Mae's mother, Nell, would know. Surely it would be before the killing frost.

But in the brightness of the morning sun, the barterman seemed like a small worry. Even the hoodoo man didn't seem worth bothering about. Black-eyed Susans nodded by the side of the road. In an overhanging hickory tree a gray squirrel, fat and sleek for winter, dropped a nut to the ground, then chattered furiously at Clara.

Clara laughed and trotted around the last bend in the path. Annie Mae was out front sweeping the yard with a new broom. Behind her was the house, large and square and comforting. From the barn, Clara heard the cow low gently.

Annie Mae grinned when she saw Clara. "What are you doing here?" she asked.

Clara held out the empty sack. "Want to go fetch some sang with me, up on Red Owl Mountain?" Quickly she explained how she'd found it, leaving out the hoodoo man, because she didn't want Annie Mae getting upset. Besides, she believed him when he said he'd leave the sang for her.

Annie Mae's eyes lit up. "Let me just finish this

sweeping or Momma will skin me alive." Dust and pebbles began flying through the air as she swished the broom back and forth. Annie Mae's father made dozens of brooms every fall from the broomcorn he planted in a hollow nearby. The barterman said they were the strongest brooms in the county.

Nell appeared on the porch, coughing and flapping her hand back and forth in front of her face. "What's ailing you, Annie Mae? Stop that right now—that dust is blowing into the house." Annie Mae's twin brothers, Joshua and Aaron, tumbled out onto the porch like two puppies. When they caught sight of Clara, they disappeared behind Nell. Clara figured they were the shyest boys she had ever laid eyes on. Even though they were four, they wouldn't talk to anybody but each other and their mother.

"Why hello there, Clara," Nell said. "How you fixing?"

"Good morning," said Clara. "I'm just fine, thank you."

"And your family?" Nell took each boy by the hand and came down off the porch.

"Daddy's gone down to Hickory Flat to do some work there," Clara answered.

Nell nodded. "I heard he was going."

"And Bessie's got a fever."

"Is she bad off?"

"No, ma'am. She'll be right as rain in no time." Clara had seen Bessie get sick like this before. She would be all right in a day or two. Then Momma would stop worrying. Just the same, Clara drew a circle in the dirt with her toe. She kept her head down, watching her foot carefully so Nell couldn't see how bad she felt about taking Bessie out in the rain.

"Momma, soon as I'm done sweeping, can I help Clara collect the rest of the sang she found yesterday on Red Owl Mountain?"

But Nell had already turned away. She shook the boys' hands free and swung her apron off over her head as she walked in the house.

When she reappeared a moment later, she was carrying her large, black doctor bag and a pail of fresh milk.

Clara recognized the bag. Nell always left it sitting right inside her door, full of clean supplies. "No use telling babies and sick folks to wait," she said.

"Mind the boys," Nell called to Annie Mae. "And listen for baby Henry. He's asleep in the cradle. Since Clara's Daddy isn't here, I'll just go round to her house and visit Lucille. She might be wanting help with Bessie."

She started up the path, then turned around. "Annie Mae, I'm expecting Miss Ella's baby to come any time now. You come get me if I'm needed, you hear?"

"Yes'm," said Annie Mae. She looked over at Clara and shrugged helplessly. Clara would have to go by herself.

chapter eight

Clara burst out of the woods by the barn holding the burlap sack. All four of the sang plants had been sitting right there in the ground, almost like they were waiting for her. It had taken only a few minutes to collect them. Then she had practically run down the mountain, her feet light as the wind.

She dashed up on the porch. But even before she opened the door she could feel something wrong. The air was thicker all of a sudden.

Bessie was lying on the big bed, and Momma was

wiping her down with a rag. She didn't seem to hear Clara come in.

Clara laid the sang on the table next to the pail of milk from Nell, then stepped quietly over to the bed.

Momma was startled when Clara appeared next to her. "Oh, Sugarcake," was all she said.

The undershirt was on the table, unfinished. Bessie lay on her back in just her new underpants. Her head fell over to one side, eyes half-open. Her chest was going up and down as she breathed, as if she had run all the way home from the woods.

Clara dropped to her knees in front of her sister. "Lil Bits?"

Bessie's eyes opened. They glittered like sun bouncing off water. It made Clara nervous.

"I got the sang," she whispered.

"Watch out," Bessie said. Her voice was high and shrill.

"What?" asked Clara. The sound of Bessie's voice made her step back. But Bessie's gaze drifted away.

"Where's Nell, Momma?" Clara couldn't stop

staring at Bessie. She'd never seen her sick like this.

"Gone home to make up some feverfew syrup," Momma said.

"Want me to take a turn wiping Bessie down?"

"That's all right, Sugarcake. But you could see if she will take a glass of milk."

Clara poured the smooth, creamy milk into a cup. A dull pain seized her stomach, and she realized she had eaten only a biscuit all day.

Carefully she carried the full cup over to the bed. But when she held the milk up to Bessie's lips, Bessie just turned away.

"It's milk, Bessie. From Annie Mae's cow." Clara looked at Momma in alarm. Bessie loved fresh milk if she could get it. Last June 'teenth Granny traded a family in town a string of fresh sunfish for a bucket of milk. Bessie drank cupfuls of it till her stomach stuck out and she fell asleep on the porch. Granny laughed and said she looked like a greedy kitten.

"Drink the milk, Clara, then fetch me some fresh spring water," said Momma. "The water in the barrels ain't very cold."

Clara drank the milk in huge gulps. "Momma,

what's the matter with Bessie?" The thickness she had felt on the porch was inside the cabin now.

"She's feverish, and she's got a sore throat. This morning she said her knees and elbows hurt."

Clara pushed away her fearful thoughts and comforted herself with Momma's words. Just a fever, that's all. Momma said so. She picked up the bucket and walked around behind the house. Just a few yards up the hill was the spring box. Daddy had built four wooden sides around the natural spring so there was always a deep place to draw water from.

Clara filled the bucket. When she carried it back inside, she found Momma in the rocking chair, holding Bessie. Nell was kneeling beside her, rummaging in her doctor bag. Nell took out Watkin's Salve and rubbed it onto Bessie's chest.

Quietly, Clara set the bucket down, the strong smell of menthol-camphor reaching her. She didn't know what to do, so she sat on her bed and watched. Nell was shaking her head back and forth. "We got to bring this fever down," she muttered.

After a few minutes of rubbing, Nell pulled a red

glass bottle out of her bag. "Here's the feverfew leaves and honey," she said. "Fetch me a spoon, Clara."

When Nell tried to spoon some into Bessie's mouth, she clenched her teeth tight and shook her head side to side.

Momma took the spoon. "Now listen to me, Lil Bits. You take Nell's medicine." Momma was using her no-nonsense voice. She wedged the spoon in between Bessie's teeth and tipped it up.

Bessie's eyes flew open and she swallowed. A trickle of the medicine ran down her chin and along her neck.

"Hello?" Annie Mae's voice came from the doorway.

"Come in," called Momma.

"Good afternoon, Mrs. Raglan," said Annie Mae. She turned to her mother. "Momma, Miss Ella is fixing to have her baby. Her husband's looking for you."

"Good. We been waiting on that baby for ten days now. Go back home, Annie Mae, and tell Miss Ella's husband I'm coming directly."

As Annie Mae ran out, Nell spoke to Momma. "You know trouble can only knock you to your knees. That's as good a place for praying as any." She dropped down to her knees beside Bessie. Her hands made a little slap as she pressed her palms together.

"Oh Lord," she began, "come help your little baby. She's needing your blessing now, sure enough."

"That's right," said Momma. She closed her eyes and began rocking Bessie gently from side to side.

"Don't be too slow, Lord," said Nell, her voice singsong. "Send your son, the Blessed Jesus, to watch over this little child of yours. You tell him not to bother to take the road, just come straight through the woods."

Watching Nell and Momma praying gave Clara the same good feeling she had listening to the preacher on Sundays. And didn't Momma say that God helps those who help themselves? They were giving Bessie herbs, and now calling on God.

"You are a lamp in the darkness, Lord," said Nell.

"Sweet Jesus," Momma called out. "Amen!"

Nell rose to her feet. "I'm sorry to leave you.

Make sure Bessie gets more of the feverfew in her now, and then give her two spoonfuls every hour or so."

Clara ran her hand down Bessie's arm. She'd be feeling better right quick.

"Soon as Miss Ella has her baby, I'll be back to check on Bessie. Pray God, I won't be too long, but this is Miss Ella's first baby."

"We'll be all right, Nell," Momma murmured. Her eyes had a prayerful feeling.

"I know you will. Still and all, I promise to be back soon as I can."

Clara followed Nell out to the porch.

"Did you find the sang?" Nell asked over her shoulder as she headed down the path.

"Yes'm," Clara called, although she could tell that Nell was already thinking ahead to Miss Ella's baby.

Clara stood on the porch, the afternoon sun warming her feet. She wasn't in any hurry to go back in.

Off to one side she saw Blackberry slip into the tall field grass, out by the covered pig pot. Clara walked over to where the hen had disappeared. She dropped gently to her knees and parted the grass. There was Blackberry sitting on the ground, her head between her shoulders, eyes closed.

"Found you, Blackberry," whispered Clara.

Blackberry's eyes opened. She tipped her head and looked sideways at Clara. *"Brrrr,"* she said softly, deep in her chest. She fluffed out her green-black feathers. Clara reached out and stroked the hen's back.

She slid her hand under the hen, palm up. Blackberry rose slightly, shuffled her feet in the grass, then settled back down onto Clara's hand. The eggs on the ground pressed into the back of her hand. Almost a full nest.

Clara nearly held her breath, she was so still. She'd tried this before, but it had never worked. The black hen looked at Clara, her yellow eyes quizzical. Then she looked at the grasses sticking up around her and plucked at one with her beak. It pulled loose, and she tucked it under her chest, right onto Clara's hand.

"I know what you are doing, Blackberry," Clara whispered. "You're pretending you're not ready to lay your egg. I can wait as long as I have to."

She settled back. Blackberry gathered more grass stems, then slowly closed her eyes. Through Blackberry's soft feathers, Clara could feel her belly tighten and soften, tighten and soften.

The sun was warm on her head and shoulders. A fly buzzed next to her ear for the longest time, then flew off. Clara's leg cramped up, and she thought she was going to have to stand, when she felt Blackberry's belly tighten harder. All the feathers on the hen's neck suddenly stuck way out. She gave a little gasp, and a warm, damp egg dropped into Clara's hand.

Blackberry got to her feet, shook herself off, and ran back to the other hens.

Clara held the egg up and watched the dampness disappear. Somehow the egg seemed full of hope. Just wait till she showed Bessie.

In the cabin Momma was sitting in the rocking chair, holding a wet rag on Bessie's forehead. The fever had turned her tawny cheeks a dusky red-brown.

"Lil Bits, look!" She held the egg up in front of

Bessie and gently touched her shoulder. Bessie's skin felt hot and dry, like the side of a woodburning stove. Clara pulled her hand back.

Bessie stared at Clara, her eyes glittery and unfocused.

Clara drew in a breath. "Blackberry laid this egg in my hand, Lil Bits. Right in my hand." She was trying to reach her sister, hidden somewhere behind all that terrible glittering.

Bessie flung out her arm, knocking the egg onto the floor. "Look out!" she cried. "Snakes! Snakes are crawling all around." She pulled up her legs. "They're going to bite us! Make them stop, please Daddy, make them stop." Her voice ended in a moan, and she slumped back, then suddenly sat straight up.

"Watch out, Granny!" She looked straight at Clara. "Why aren't you listening to me, Granny? There's a copperhead by your foot, going to bite you!"

Clara stepped back onto the broken egg. It was wet and slimy on the sole of her foot, but she barely noticed.

"What's wrong with Bessie, Momma?"

"She's gone out of her head with the fever." Momma's eyes were wide with fear. "Quick, get fresh spring water. We need it cold as we can get."

"Daddy! Daddy!" Bessie was half moaning, half demanding. "There's a rattler, Daddy, as big as your arm. Don't you see him curling up, getting ready to strike? He's rattling his tail, rattling so loud!" She threw her hands up over her ears.

Clara grabbed the bucket and ran out the door. She lay on her stomach in front of the spring and forced the bucket down as deep as she could reach. The cold water made her arm ache. As she ran back, the water splashed down her legs and feet.

She rounded the side of the house, and something inside her broke open. The fullness of her fears washed through her. Did Old Sugar do this? Make Bessie all glittery-eyed, seeing snakes and people that weren't really there? Clara's legs nearly buckled underneath her.

Momma had Bessie back on the big bed. She beckoned Clara to her side. "Quick," she said, "wet these rags and cover her with them."

Clara plunged the rags into the bucket and drew

them up, dripping. She shook one loose and tried to wring it out. Her hands were trembling so hard she could barely make them work.

Bessie suddenly sat up, like a puppet pulled by strings. "There's a big one," she moaned, "coming right for me. Let me ride on your shoulders, Daddy. Get me away from the snakes." Her voice dropped, and she began whimpering. "Why don't you come get me, Daddy?" Abruptly she rose to her knees, flipped over, and tried to burrow into the mattress.

"Hush, Lil Bits, hush," said Momma. She pulled Bessie into her lap and held her tightly. "Get those wet rags on her, Clara." Shaking and crying, Clara put the rags all over Bessie. Bessie continued to moan and talk, but her voice dropped to a low mutter. Clara couldn't understand what she was saying. As Clara pulled off rags, wet them, and put them back on, Bessie slowly became more still.

Finally Clara sat down, breathing heavily. She held dripping wet rags in both hands. Momma was soaked. Water was everywhere.

Momma leaned over and put Bessie down on the big bed. The dime swung freely from Momma's neck, glimmering in the soft light. The glimmering frightened Clara, but at least the dime hadn't tarnished.

Bessie lay with her eyes closed. Momma smoothed Bessie's hair, tucking loose ends into her braids. "You see what that hoodoo man did to my baby?"

"Momma?" Clara's voice came out in a squeak.

"You should never have talked with that two-shadow man."

Clara could feel the shame rising up from her chest, filling her head, drumming in her ears. She took the fullness of Momma's blame. She'd done one thing wrong after another, starting with breaking the crock. And this is where it had led, right to her sister's terrible, swift sickness.

Momma leaned forward. "Why didn't you run . . ."

Clara pointed at Momma's neck. "The dime, Momma."

Momma grabbed the dime. "What?"

"It ain't tarnished."

Momma peered at the dime. She gasped. "Still shiny!"

Momma's face crumpled like it was falling from the inside out. "What if he's so good at hoodoo he could put a fix on one of us and it wouldn't show up on my dime?"

She began crying, a deep, painful sobbing that Clara had never heard before. It sounded like someplace in Momma had been torn wide open. The sound of her sobbing filled the little cabin, making Bessie stir on the bed.

Clara felt the rags in her hands dripping cold water down the sides of her legs. She couldn't move, she couldn't think. She might have stood that way for minutes, or she might have stood that way for hours.

Finally Momma's crying softened. She raised her head. Her eyes were swollen. "Why is Bessie sick?" she whispered.

Clara wasn't sure if Momma was talking out loud to herself or asking her. She waited a moment, then spoke.

"I don't know, Momma," she said into the emptiness. "Maybe Nell will know what to do when she comes back."

"Can't wait," said Momma. "Can't wait." Suddenly she slapped her hand down hard on the table. In the stillness of the cabin, it sounded like a rifle shot. "I'm going for the white doctor."

Relief ran though Clara. Of course, the white doctor! Hadn't he set Annie Mae's leg when she fell off her mule and broke it, and now it was good as new? And when Mr. Jones had milk fever, he'd cured him. The white doctor lived in town, just at the south end. Clara passed his house when she walked to school. Momma had never gone for him before, but she'd never needed to.

But then a new worry came rushing at Clara, pushing aside her relief. "What if Bessie goes out of her head again while you're gone?" She didn't want to be left alone with her sister who was not her sister.

"Then you'll need to put cold cloths on her," said Momma. She took one of the rags and wiped off her face. Then she was gone.

chapter nine

Clara couldn't bear to sit next to Bessie on the big bed. Instead, she sat at the table. She closed her eyes and watched Momma in her mind. She'd walk alongside the creek a little ways, then follow the path through the woods. It wouldn't take her long to get to Annie Mae's house, not more than fifteen or twenty minutes. Maybe Momma would holler just to make sure Nell wasn't home, even though Momma would know she wasn't. She'd walk, quickly now, down the path where it fell steeply to the valley floor. There she'd turn left, heading north into town on the wide dirt road, heading straight for the doctor's house. If the doctor was home, he'd saddle up his horse and come right along.

Much, much farther away, Daddy was working in Hickory Flat. He'd be in a barn, his big piece of leather spread out over his knee, a harness or bridle across his lap. Maybe he was stretching out his tired shoulders or rubbing his fingers that grew stiff from pushing the big needles through leather all day. If only he knew, he would be hurrying back, coming up Greyland Road as fast as he could. In her mind she called out to him, *Hurry home, Daddy. Bessie is mighty sick. Maybe even dying, Daddy.*

She glanced over at Bessie. Still sleeping. Clara's mind started skipping lightly, like a stone across a pond. Hurry, Momma, bring the white doctor. Come home, Daddy. Come back, Nell. Clara looked through the open door and waited, waited for someone to come save Bessie. Outside, the late afternoon light was turning pink and rich and full. A light wind rustled through the treetops. Clara thought it sounded like angels unfurling their wings, getting

ready to fly across the sky under God's watch-
ful eye. "Come see to Bessie," she murmured.

Buckshot brayed from across the creek. Clara
snapped awake. Through the open door she saw
the white doctor riding up on his gray mare, his long
legs dangling down. Momma was walking next to him.

The doctor tied his horse to the corner post of
the porch and took long, striding steps into the
cabin. He stood blinking in the soft light. Clara
could see the outline of his battered hat, his narrow
shoulders, and his doctoring bag. He reminded her
of the tall, thin cranes that stood on one leg in the
creek, spearing frogs with their beaks.

The doctor swept off his hat. "Where's the sick
child?" he asked. His voice was surprisingly slow
for someone who moved in such a quick, nervous
way.

Momma slipped in behind him.

Clara jumped to her feet and ran over to the bed.
"Here," she answered.

The doctor dropped his black bag on the floor.
In the quiet of the cabin it made a loud thump.
He drew his bushy eyebrows together and stared

down at Bessie, then knelt in front of her.

Momma came up next to Clara and put a hand on her shoulder, steadying herself. She was still breathing hard from walking back up the mountain.

"Hello, child," the white doctor said to Bessie.

When she didn't respond, he used his thumb to gently roll back her eyelid. Bessie startled and opened both eyes. She stared at the doctor. Bessie's eyes weren't shiny anymore, but dull and unseeing.

The doctor placed his hands on Bessie's belly, feeling all over with swift, firm movements. How pale his hands looked against her tawny skin.

As the doctor pressed on her stomach, Bessie twisted and gave a soft moan. Clara watched fearfully, but the doctor was done quickly.

"She was out of her mind with fever," said Momma.

"For how long?"

"Wasn't too long. We brought the fever down with wet rags." She looked at Clara. "When I was gone . . . did she . . ."

Clara shook her head. "No, Momma, she slept the whole time."

The doctor felt under Bessie's arms, then ran the palm of his hand over her shoulders, elbows, and knees. Bessie groaned again and tried feebly to push the doctor's hands away. Momma sat on the bed by Bessie's feet and took her hands. "Hush, Lil Bits. He's here to help."

"Inflammation in the joints," the doctor muttered. He put his ear to Bessie's chest and listened. Clara saw his blue eyes were kind and a bit sad. "Heart going like galloping horses."

Clara could see Momma searching the doctor's face for clues about what was wrong with Bessie. She knew Momma wouldn't mention about hoodoo. She would just hope he could heal her. But Clara wanted Momma to ask something, anything, to find out more.

Carefully the doctor ran his hands under Bessie's chin. He pulled a flat stick out of his bag and looked down her throat.

Bessie gagged and started whimpering again.

Clara wished Bessie would holler like she usually did when someone bothered her. Her whimpering reminded Clara of a kitten she saw last winter. It was so skinny she could see its ribs under the thin, dry fur. It stood by the side of the road, not knowing if it should run, giving a pitiful cry. Clara had paused uncertainly, wishing she could help. Finally she broke off part of her cornbread and left a piece by the road. Then she ran, ran as fast as she could, to put the thin crying behind her.

The doctor snapped his bag open. "Bad case of mountain fever," he said. "Comes on mighty fast."

He thrust his hands into his doctoring bag and pulled out two hollow glass balls about the size of apples. On the side of each ball was a round opening. "We'll cup her," he said.

Clara saw her mother nod, tight-lipped.

The doctor took out a small red bottle and wrenched the cork out with his teeth. Then he gripped a small cotton rag with a pair of tweezers and poured alcohol onto it. As soon as he held a match to the cotton, it burst into flame. Moving swiftly, he put the flaming cotton to the opening in the glass ball. A moment later he pulled out the cotton, then tipped the open side of the glass against the inside of Bessie's elbow. It stuck tight, pulling her skin up into it.

"This will take the poisons out of the joint," he said, as he fixed the second cup to her other elbow. "As the heat from the alcohol fire cools off, the air inside pulls her skin in. See how it's getting red? That's the poisons coming out."

Momma was nodding, just nodding her head up and down. Clara didn't think she was hearing a word the doctor said. At least the cupping didn't seem to hurt Bessie. She wasn't moaning or trying to push the doctor's hands away.

He waited a few moments, then pulled off the cups. They left round red marks on Bessie's skin. Lighting and relighting the cotton, he fixed the cups to her shoulders, and then her knees.

Clara watched in amazement. So this was the white doctor's cure for Bessie's sickness. Would it take hoodoo poison out of her? Or only mountain fever?

The doctor took a large brown bottle out of his bag and poured something pale on several long strips of rag. Then he spread the strips with a greasy salve and wrapped them around Bessie's elbows, knees, and shoulders. Clara could smell the sharp odor of turpentine mixed with lard.

"The fever is carried on the mountain wind," the doctor said. "Some catch it, others don't. She needs to drink as often as possible. Water is fine. Keep her cool as you can."

He put everything back in his bag and looked at Momma. "I'm afraid the fever can just burn her right up. A white boy died from it yesterday in Owen's Valley."

Clara felt Momma sway.

"You don't mean Bessie's going to die?" Clara blurted out. "Are you sure Bessie's got mountain fever? It ain't nothing else?"

He nodded. "It's mountain fever, all right. I see a lot of it right now. Comes almost every fall."

"And you've seen it come on this fast?" Clara was standing so close to the doctor she could see tiny yellow flecks in his blue eyes. "With folks getting out of their heads like Bessie?"

Could sickness really move this fast, Clara wondered, or only hoodoo sickness?

"It's unfortunate she's been delirious. That happens when the fever shoots up quick. If her fever breaks by morning, she'll probably make it."

Momma put her hand on Clara's arm and stared at her in disbelief. Clara wasn't sure if it was because she had been so outspoken with the doctor, or if it was what he was saying about Bessie.

"Clara, go get the doctor a couple of hens—good layers." Momma's words were hard and tight, like they didn't all fit together. "And one or two of them old stewing hens."

Clara grabbed a burlap bag from the shelf and ran outside. Behind the mountains, the sun was falling. Its dying rays edged the white clouds in a fierce and blinding gold. The sky was streaked with red and pink and orange. It looked like all of heaven was on fire. Clara put her head down and ran.

The chickens were waiting restlessly to be let into the henhouse for the night. She grabbed two old stewing hens and a young layer and stuffed them into the bag. The rest of the flock stood in front of her, fidgety and nervous. She needed one more good layer. Smack in the middle was Blackberry, tipping her head at Clara and staring at her with bright yellow eyes.

Clara dove headfirst into the flock. She grabbed Blackberry by the leg. She'd get rid of her. Give her to the doctor.

She scrambled to her feet, holding Blackberry upside down in one hand, the burlap bag in the other. Blackberry's wings fell open, and her head hung down loosely.

From behind her, the doctor spoke. "Three's enough."

Clara heard his words, but they didn't make sense in her head. Three what? And what was enough? Nothing was enough right now. Nothing would ever be enough if Bessie died.

She swung Blackberry toward the sack to shove her in. The hen twisted frantically in Clara's hand, beating her wings uselessly. As Clara tried again to thrust her in, Blackberry stretched her neck out stiff, then suddenly went limp, her eyes shutting.

"Blackberry!" Clara cried. Everything seemed to go so slow, there almost wasn't a next moment. Out of the corner of her eye she glimpsed a barn swallow, a dark shape against the pink-and-red sunset-filled sky. The swallow seemed to be poised, perfectly still, before swooping through the sky and disappearing behind the barn.

"It's all right," said the doctor. "The hen's just stunned, on account of being held upside down. Let her go."

Clara pulled Blackberry back. She thrust the sack full of hens at the doctor and cradled Blackberry to her chest. She didn't feel her own crying till she saw clear, wet drops hit Blackberry's feathers and roll off.

"I'm sorry, I'm sorry," she whispered. Blackberry's head hung limply over her arm, her beak open and her small, pointed tongue showing. Clara slipped her fingers under Blackberry's feathers and felt the warm skin of the hen's body. Fast, tiny heartbeats drummed against her fingertips.

She turned and ran past the doctor, down through the field. Surely, she thought, surely all the angels are weeping now. She didn't stop till she was at the creek, kneeling on the twisted roots of the willow trees.

Clara dipped her hand in the water, then let a few drops slide from her wet fingers onto the hen's tongue. A second and third time she dripped water into Blackberry's mouth. Suddenly the hen sneezed, water flying out of the tiny nose holes in her beak. She brought her head up and peered uncertainly at Clara.

With a motion soft as thistledown falling, Clara set Blackberry on the ground. The hen rose unsteadily to her feet. Then she shook herself and took off for the rest of the flock.

Clara watched Blackberry's rolling, jerky run. She wanted to run herself, run all the way to the woods, throw herself under a tree, and stay there till . . . till what? Till Bessie got better. If Bessie got better.

Clara grabbed the old, gnarly bark of the willow root with one hand. She stared at the swirling green water of the creek. Was it just yesterday morning that Momma had been down here washing out the crocks? It seemed like a long, long time ago.

chapter ten

Inside, Momma had lit the lamp. Bessie lay sleeping on the big bed. Her eyes seemed sunken deeper in her head, with a shadowy darkness around them.

Momma sat at the table humming, sad and low. Almost more like a moaning. The sound hollowed out Clara, leaving her empty and achy.

She stood in front of Momma. "Are you hungry?" she asked.

Momma shook her head.

"Thirsty?"

"I believe I am." A tired smile passed across Momma's face.

Clara drew a dipperful of water from the bucket near the fireplace. It seemed like the shadows were crouching in the corners, waiting for death to creep in.

Momma drank thirstily.

"More, Momma?"

"No thank you."

Bessie whimpered, and Momma gathered her up in her arms. Bessie was limp as a dishrag. Momma sat on the edge of the bed, rocking and singing gently. She had her head back and her eyes closed.

> *Pray on,*
> *Pray on,*
> *We'll meet you on the other side.*

Did Momma know what she was singing? Clara wondered. When Clara was little, maybe about Bessie's age, Granny had come to visit in June, like she did every year. One night on the porch, Granny was mourning and singing "pray on" 'cause her oldest friend, Haddy, had died. Granny told Clara it was the song they used to sing in slavery times when a slave was sold away. "I lost two of my children that way—my two oldest," she said. "Sold away. You'd never see them no more till you were standing in front of God."

For a minute Granny's eyes were looking back in time, and sorrow weighed down her shoulders. Then she turned and grinned at Clara. "But I searched them out, after the War between the States was over, and we had our freedom. Took me three years, but I found them both. Glory, glory!"

"Bring me more water, Sugarcake. Let's see if Bessie will drink."

Clara fetched another dipper of water. She tipped it up to Bessie's lips, but the water just ran down her chin.

"Pass me the undershirt I was sewing," Momma whispered.

Clara handed it to her. Momma slipped a corner of the cloth in the dipper and tucked the wet fabric into Bessie's mouth. At first Bessie turned away, then she began weakly sucking.

"Praise the Lord," said Momma softly.

Clara felt her knees go weak with relief. At least Bessie was drinking.

Bessie took water three more times before she quit sucking.

Clara sat down and leaned her cheek on the table.

"When will Nell come back, Momma?"

"There must be some trouble with that baby. She'll be here soon as she can."

Clara had a terrible feeling it might be too late. But she didn't say so. She could tell that Momma had the same thought. What was unspoken hung unbearably between them.

Clara jumped to her feet and went to the window. Up on the mountainside, Old Sugar's light went on.

Clara thought back to meeting him on Red Owl Mountain. She remembered the plants he had collected, and the herbs for root medicine. He had even offered her a piece of his devil's shoestring to keep the snakes away.

The devil's shoestring. Bessie had taken it and put it in her pocket.

There was a rushing sound in Clara's ears. Fear swirled over her, like the time she was fishing with Daddy and fell into the creek. The water had pulled her under, tumbling her over and over until she grabbed onto a willow root. She had held on, coughing and gasping and crying, till Daddy had pulled her out.

"Clara?" said Momma. "You look like a ghost just walked across your grave."

Clara glanced at Momma's dime, ghostly silver in the lamplight. Momma would know if the hoodoo man could have put a fix on Bessie with the devil's shoestring. But she couldn't tell Momma. Clara looked at Bessie's dress hanging on a nail over their bed. In the pocket, right over where she and Bessie slept last night, was the slender root.

Momma came and stood next to her, staring at the pinprick of light. "That hoodoo man is the cause of all our troubles right now," she said bitterly.

"But when we saw him a few days ago . . . he told

us about root medicine, and how to keep snakes away. . . ."

"Listen at me, Clara. It's time you understood. One of those hoodoo men took my momma. But they're not going to get my baby."

"Why?" Clara shuddered. "Why would someone hoodoo your momma?" She had never heard this before.

"I don't know why, Clara. I never found out. I was little when my momma died. Folks said Momma got sick because of the bad swamp air around our house. But Miss Tilly, our neighbor, finally let on she heard it was hoodoo. Said she saw the sack and everything."

Momma shook her head. "I remember it like it was yesterday. For the longest time Momma lay in that bed, wasting away. Eating was hard, then it got so she could only drink. One day I came home, and Miss Tilly had covered up the little mirror that hung over the bed. Momma was dead."

"But it wasn't this hoodoo man, was it?"

"No, it happened long ago."

"I ain't scared of this hoodoo man," said Clara, although her heart was pounding.

"Lord have mercy, Clara. Saying you're not afraid of hoodoo!"

"I'll go ask him, Momma!" Clara said wildly. "If he put a fix on Bessie, I'll tell him to take it off."

"It's more than an hour of walking to get down the valley and up the other side to Old Sugar's." Momma's voice was harsh. "And there's haunts all over the road at night. I'm losing Bessie and I'm not losing you, too. Bessie's in God's hands now." A wrenching noise—half-sob, half-howl—escaped from deep in Momma's throat.

"Now, go close the shutters. It's time for bed."

There was something so final in Momma's words that all the arguing went out of Clara. She slipped onto the porch and pulled the heavy wooden shutters closed. Out in the dark, she felt a terrible relief that Momma wouldn't let her go for the hoodoo man. What if Momma had said yes, go, hurry. Could she have?

Clara stood on the porch, breathing heavily. Over in the field, one firefly flickered, then another. Bessie loved those fireflies. Maybe she could catch her one.

Clara listened carefully for sounds of any haunts calling her name. But all she heard were the frogs by the creek. She hesitated a moment, then walked quickly into the field. She faced the house, trying to stay in the long path of light that poured out from the open door.

She made herself stay out in the dark until she had caught two fireflies. Cupping them gently in her hands, she saw them glow between her fingers as they flashed on and off. Softly, she ran inside and stood over the bed where Bessie lay sleeping. She spread her fingers wide, and the fireflies flew up into the rafters.

"They're angel lights," she whispered to Bessie, "going to watch over you tonight."

chapter eleven

Clara woke with a feeling of dread. She lay in bed, waiting without knowing why. Far across the valley, an owl gave a mournful cry. Then she remembered. Bessie.

She felt along the wall until she found her dress. She slipped it on, then reached into Bessie's pocket. Empty. In the other pocket, her fingers closed over the thin root. It felt almost alive to her. She thrust it in her own pocket and reached underneath the bed for her cigar box.

With trembling fingers she searched till she found Granny's knife. She slipped it in her pocket with the devil's shoelace. Maybe all the good in that knife would be strong enough to hold back any hoodoo in the root till she got rid of it. She was going to run down to the stream right now and throw it in there and let the water carry it away.

Clara stirred up the coals in the fireplace until a small flame sprung up. On tiptoe she crept over to the big bed. By the flickering light she could see Bessie sprawled out, covers pushed aside. Her breath was light and panting. It looked like her spirit was hiding deep inside her now, not filling her up like it should. Momma lay behind Bessie, one arm thrown over her eyes. Behind them on the wall, Clara's shadow danced nervously. She touched Bessie's cheek. Hot and dry. She was burning up, just like the doctor said.

The owl called again, closer this time. Clara shivered. Everyone knew if an owl lit on your house, someone inside was going to die. She slipped out onto the porch.

Rivers of silvery stars flowed across the black sky. In the crisp autumn air they glimmered and called to her. If only she could fly off the edge of the porch and gather armfuls and armfuls. Surely they would heal Bessie.

Suddenly the owl swept in, heading toward the cabin. Clara heard the *whoosh-whoosh-whoosh* of its huge wings as it came closer. The stars disappeared, as if the owl were devouring them, then reappeared as it flew nearer. Above the roof the owl pumped its wings backward to land. Clara saw the outline of its sharp talons.

"No!" she hissed, flinging out her arms. "You can't take my little sister!" She leapt wildly off the edge of the porch and tumbled onto the dusty ground.

Startled, the owl banked and flew off the way it had come. Clara crouched in the dust, trembling like a little wild rabbit.

When the owl was gone, she scrambled to her feet. Beneath the shining stars, the world was dark and waiting.

Just beyond where she could sense, there were sure to be haunts. They'd be hiding under the trees by the path, walking along the road, moaning and shaking their chains. Haunts who could catch her by the ankle and whirl her over to the other side.

And past the road, up the other side of the valley, was the hoodoo man.

Gazing up, with nothing between her and the bright shiny stars, Clara knew what to do. She wouldn't throw the root away. She'd carry it to the hoodoo man and make him take off the fix. And if he hadn't put a fix on Bessie, maybe his herb medicine could help. Clara took a shuddery breath. She was the one who got Bessie into this trouble. Now she had to get her out.

She ran past Momma's garden and over to the barn. Warm, sweet air pressed against her arms and face as she opened the door.

She slipped inside the stall where Buckshot stood sleeping. "Wake up," she said, tugging on his mane. "We got to go see Old Sugar."

Buckshot swung his big head around and put his chin on her shoulder. He gave a soft, welcoming bray, and his whiskers tickled her neck. Clara slipped his bridle on and led him outside. Maybe up on his wide back she wouldn't be so easy for the haunts to grab.

Walking out into the field, she could just make out

the shadowy shape of the pig pot, humped over and brooding in the darkness. Why hadn't she thought to get a candle stub out of her box? But she didn't dare go back now.

"You be quiet, Buckshot," she whispered as she led the mule down the path toward the creek. "If you wake Momma, she's sure to stop me." Clara looked across the valley and up the mountainside, wishing Old Sugar's light was on so she could find him.

The way she figured it, Old Sugar was straight across the valley from them, only higher up. She'd have to ride down past Annie Mae's house to the dirt road that ran along the valley floor. Where Momma had turned left to get to town to fetch the doctor, she'd have to go right. Then it wouldn't be far till she would need to find a way up the mountain.

Momma had said it would take more than an hour. The moon wasn't up yet, so she hadn't been sleeping that long. Not more than an hour or two. Pray God, she had time to get to Old Sugar's and get home before dawn.

Clara led Buckshot over to a black walnut stump and stepped up. Granny's knife thumped gently against her thigh as she threw herself across Buckshot's back. Her fears were running every whichaway, filling her up. A wave of pity ran through her, and she thought longingly of her warm bed. Then she stiffened up and told Buckshot to get moving. If Granny could see her now, she'd think she was pitiful.

A light wind blew the dampness off the water as the path wound next to the creek. Clara shivered in her thin cotton dress. At least Buckshot was warm beneath her.

The path narrowed as they left the creek and headed downhill. Then they rounded a bend, and she could no longer look back and see the meadow. From now on, she would be in the dark woods. The trees closed around her, swaying and groaning in the night breeze. She tried to keep them from feeling like tall, muttering haunts, but the wind was filling them with life.

A thistle scratched Clara's bare calf. With a jerk, she pulled her legs up. What if a haunt stuck a bony hand out of the bushes and grabbed her ankle?

"This is the same path I always take to Annie Mae's house," she told Buckshot. She knew she was talking out loud just to feel brave, but she didn't care. Somewhere beyond the trees, the moon was rising, making the sky lighter. It made the trees seem larger and more frightening.

"We're almost there, Buckshot, it's just down this straight part of the path, then two more curves." Talking was better than being quiet and listening. As she talked she ran her fingers through Buckshot's mane, concentrating on undoing snarls and pulling out little burrs.

"The house is coming up," she said after they went around the first bend. "I've gone on this path hundreds of times, going to Annie Mae's, then going on to school."

When she rounded the second curve, she was so surprised that she jerked Buckshot to a stop. The house was gone. Where there should have been a clearing and a low fence, all Clara saw were the dark shapes of trees pressing against the path. Her skin suddenly felt tight all over.

She urged Buckshot forward, straining her eyes in the darkness. Where was Annie Mae's house? Could the haunts get her lost? She thought back quickly. She'd come straight down the path, just like she always did. She couldn't be lost. But her heart beat hard with fear. She knew the path so well, yet it seemed different in the dark. Maybe it was farther to Annie Mae's.

"Go on," she said wildly to Buckshot. "Keep going. We'll find it." Buckshot flicked his big ears backward and forward, listening to her.

Just around the next bend was the house. Clara pulled Buckshot up in front and took deep, gulping breaths of air. Annie Mae was sleeping in there, with her father and the twins and the baby. For a minute she thought of waking the whole family and getting Annie Mae's father to go with her, but she quickly laid that idea aside. He might make her wait for Nell. And she couldn't wait. Thinking of Nell gave Clara a strange kind of comfort. It felt good knowing Nell was awake, even if she was in town waiting for Miss Ella to have her baby.

As Clara lingered, not wanting to leave, a three-quarter moon cleared the trees. Its ivory white smoothness reminded her of the earthenware crock.

She slapped Buckshot's reins lightly across his neck, and he started into a slow walk. The path fell steeply to the valley floor, and the moonlight made deep shadows under the trees. At least before, everything had been dark.

Clara snapped her head from side to side, frightened of what could be hiding in the shadows. Granny always told Clara to be careful on a moonshiny night or she'd hear haunts playing ghostly fiddles. Once you heard their unearthly music, your feet would get to dancing and you couldn't stop for anything. With that music playing faster and faster, they could dance you right into death.

Clara rubbed her shivering arms, trying to push the coldness out of them. Leastways, she thought it was cold that was making her shiver. She hadn't realized how cold the nights were now. That killing frost was sure to come soon.

The path spilled abruptly onto the dirt road into town. Clara hesitated. She had never followed the road to the right. Others took it, like Granny, and Daddy, going to Hickory Flat. And now her. She turned the mule down the road, away from town.

As the mule walked, Clara stared into the trees crowding the side of the road, searching for a path up the slope. But all she saw were wild plum trees and the round, bursting petals of the black-eyed Susans. What if she walked and walked and never found a path? Maybe she had come all this way for nothing.

She began combing her fingers through Buckshot's mane again. "You've been to Old Sugar's before, with Daddy. You've got to get us back up there. Please, Buckshot." He tossed his head and blew out hard, as if he were listening.

Finally she spotted a break in the trees, a narrow emptiness leading up the mountain. Was this it? A sharp stab of fear made her tighten her belly. It looked like a deer trail. But Old Sugar wouldn't need much to come and go, seeing as how he didn't even have a mule.

"Well, go on," she said fiercely, kicking Buckshot in the sides. She had to try something, or daylight was going to find her here, wondering what to do.

The mule jerked as he took his first step, then climbed steadily up the mountain. Clara felt his muscles bunch and strain as they went higher and higher.

A sharp gust of wind blew through the trees. They leaned and swayed, rubbing against one another. In her weariness Clara heard a new sound: fiddles playing high, fretful melodies. *Cree-cree-cree* went their bows, scraping across the strings. The haunts had finally found her, alone in the woods with Buckshot.

"No!" Clara shrieked.

Buckshot lunged forward. Clara flew off backward and landed flat on her back. She stared up into the moon-washed sky and fought to take in a breath. It felt like two huge, invisible hands were squeezing her chest.

She struggled to her feet and tried to breathe in. It seemed like her front and back were stuck together, with no place inside for air. She couldn't even pull the breath down into her throat. She tried again. Nothing. Finally on her third try, she sucked in a big, cold burst of air. With a rush she let it out, and then she was taking huge, gulping breaths.

As her breathing softened, she heard the fiddle music again.

"I ain't dancing to your fiddling, 'cause I ain't listening at you," she hollered. But she did listen. Her ears felt as big as Buckshot's. Turning her head every which way, she found the *cree-cree, cree-cree* sound was coming from high in the trees. She peered up but didn't see anything. Then the wind gusted hard, and she saw the branches scraping back and forth on one another.

Her knees buckled and her body swayed. "That ain't haunts, Buckshot. It's just tree branches." She grabbed for his reins to keep from falling. "No need to be afraid."

But he kept walking up the path, away from the scraping sound.

Clara took small running steps alongside him. "Let me figure out where we are." She grabbed a handful of mane and hauled herself up on his back.

"Now stay still." She rose to her knees and then pulled herself up by his mane until she was standing on his wide back. She could see out through the trees and across the valley. She was pretty far up the mountain. They must be more than halfway to Old Sugar's. Tears sprung into her eyes, and she wiped them away with the back of her hand. This was no time for crying.

Underneath her feet, she felt Buckshot ease forward, sneaking like a barnyard cat. Quickly, she slid back down.

"All right, Buckshot," she said. "It won't be long now." She gave herself over to the steady movement of Buckshot's walk. She half-closed her eyes and let her legs dangle. Even though she was colder than she'd ever been, she felt a hazy sleep overtaking her.

A sharp rustling sound brought her back awake. Buckshot's ears pricked forward and his nostrils flared. He came to a sudden stop, his front legs splayed out.

Desperately, Clara scanned the leaves. A branch dipped and swayed, as if it had caught the weight of something.

A loud yowl came from behind the leaves.

Buckshot whinnied in fear. Clara gasped and ducked down behind his neck, the blood hammering in her ears.

Another yowl, louder this time, made her snap her head back up. It was more frightening not to look.

A cougar crouched on the swaying branch, its yellow eyes shining in the moonlight. For a heartbeat, it stared at her. Then it leapt silently to the ground and ran across the path into the trees.

Buckshot jumped straight up into the air. Clara came down on his back with such a hard thump her arms and legs flopped like a rag doll's. Underneath her, she felt Buckshot's terrified breathing. He backed into the bushes and tried to turn around, pulling at the bridle.

Clara held tight to his reins, the leather cutting into her hands. "We can't go back now. We have to get to Old Sugar's."

The mule's ears were flat back with fear, and his breath came in heaving snorts.

"That cougar is gone, Buckshot." Clara could barely speak through her chattering teeth. "I think we scared that cat as much as it scared us." She stroked the mule's neck, trying to calm herself as well.

What if that wasn't really a cougar? It might be a haunt, out prowling around, taking the shape of a cougar. Would it return and call out her name, take her over to the other side?

In a sudden, fearful rage, she pounded her heels into the mule's sides. "Go! Go as fast as you can!" She grabbed the leather reins and slapped them, as hard as she could, across his neck.

Buckshot lurched forward, timidly at first, then faster and faster. Finally he broke into a full gallop, and Clara had to hang on tight. Branches slashed at her as the path narrowed. She pulled her head down beside his neck and squeezed her eyes shut. The sound of his pounding feet filled her ears.

chapter twelve

Suddenly they burst into a clearing, coming to a stop so fast Clara almost flew over Buckshot's head. She thumped down onto his back and felt his neck muscles tighten as he raised his head and brayed, wildly, to a little cabin set in the middle of the clearing.

Buckshot pricked his big ears forward and listened. There was a terrible stillness. Even the slightest wind had quit whispering in the trees. Buckshot brayed again, louder.

Clara heard footsteps in the cabin. Suddenly

bright light poured out of the open window. "Who's there?"

Clara's spirit trembled, turned, and hid somewhere deep inside her. She pressed her knees into Buckshot's sides and held tight to his reins, keeping herself steady. Why had she come? What should she say?

Old Sugar threw open the door, and Clara saw the outline of his tall, lanky figure.

Fear made her move fast. She pulled the devil's shoelace out of her pocket and flung it on the porch. "Did you put a fix on my little sister?" She could hear a wild crying sound in her voice. She swallowed hard to keep it from bursting out and taking over.

"Clara?" He reached down and picked up the root. "You come all this way to ask me that? In the middle of the night?"

"Bessie took sick. Terrible sick. And Daddy's gone to Hickory Flat."

Old Sugar turned the devil's shoelace in his hands. "This root is just something to carry in your pocket so snakes won't bite you. Ain't nothing more." He sprung down off his low porch.

"I only work a good hand, Clara." She could hear the sorrow in his voice. "I'd lose my curing hand if I did a bad fix on anybody."

"Momma says you're the cause of all our troubles right now."

"Your momma thinks I put a fix on Bessie? Made her sick?" Even in the moonlight, his eyes had that steady, sharp foxlike look. "It's curing I'm interested in."

Clara remembered him going over all the plants he'd found up on the mountain. How much he knew. How Daddy seemed to trust him. The part she couldn't work out was Momma's fear.

"Why is Momma so scared of you?"

Old Sugar shook his head. "I don't rightly know. Folks are afraid of hoodoo. Some are even afraid of me."

"Momma said when she was coming up, her Momma died of a fix from a hoodoo man."

"Losing your momma runs deep," he said softly. "Auntie Charlotte Rose was like a momma to me. Sometimes at night I still remember little things about her, like the churning song she used to sing."

> *Come butter, come,*
> *Missus awaiting,*
> *For that butter cake to come.*

Old Sugar's eyes were faraway-looking. Then he continued softly, "She died a few years after freedom came. Losing her tore me all to pieces."

Clara reached out her hand. Old Sugar understood and handed her up the devil's shoestring. She slipped it into her pocket with Granny's knife.

"Can you tell me some herb medicine I can use to help Bessie?"

"It depends on the sickness."

"The white doctor said it was mountain fever."

"I'd have to take a look at her."

"Then come back with me," Clara said. "See for yourself."

"I have to be asked, child."

Clara thought, Ain't I asking you? But she didn't say anything.

As if he had heard her thoughts, he answered. "It's your momma. She's not going to take help from me."

How could he just give up like that, without even trying? "Don't you understand? Bessie's mighty sick, maybe dying!"

Old Sugar looked at her steadily in the moonlight. "All right," he said. "But if your momma tries to run me off, I'll have to go."

"You can tell Momma about your herb study, and your Auntie Charlotte Rose," Clara said. "You can make her understand. Hurry, please hurry." Now that Old Sugar was going to help, she had a burning desire to get back. She realized with a start she hadn't thought of her sister since she set out. She'd been so worried about haunts and hoodoo. Was Bessie even still alive?

Old Sugar led Buckshot over to a big bush and tied him there. "I need to know which herbs to bring. Tell me what you can."

So Clara told him everything, starting with Momma noticing Bessie getting hot, and then going out of her head the next day, and the white doctor cupping her. She finished up with how Bessie looked when she tiptoed out of the house a few hours ago.

Old Sugar rubbed his palm over his chin. "Rest yourself a minute while I collect a few things."

Clara threw her leg over the mule's back and slid to the ground. To her surprise, her legs didn't hold her up. Old Sugar had to grab her arm to keep her from falling.

"You're cold!" he exclaimed. Clara shrugged. She supposed she was so cold she couldn't feel it any longer. His hand felt warm and steady. He led her over to the porch and disappeared inside the cabin.

When he came back out, he handed her his wool coat. It smelled like wood smoke and dried herbs. Gratefully, she put it on and fastened the big buttons down the front. At first the coat scratched her neck, and then a thin warmth curled around her.

Clara took a deep breath and swung up on Buckshot. Old Sugar slung his tow sack over his shoulder and walked behind her as they headed down the narrow path. Clara didn't speak, and she was glad Old Sugar didn't either. She was thinking about

Bessie, as if thinking about her could keep her living. Hold on, Bessie, she said in her mind. We're coming. Just hold on.

When they got to the wide dirt road to town, she saw that the moon had moved across the sky and was beginning to arch down toward the trees. In another couple hours it would disappear behind Red Owl Mountain.

Eagerly, Buckshot walked up the road and turned onto the path home, thrusting his head forward with every step. He didn't even pause as they passed Annie Mae's house. Clara was trying to puzzle out what to say to Momma about Old Sugar. The next thing she knew, she smelled the cool green smell of water, and they were walking beside the creek.

As they rode up the field, Clara saw light coming out through the missing chinks in the walls. Her heart started pounding all over again. Why was the lamp lit? Was Bessie dead and Momma sitting up with her?

"I'd better go talk to Momma alone," Clara said. She slid off the mule, threw the reins to Old Sugar, and tore across the field, fear drumming in her ears.

"I'll settle the mule," Old Sugar called after her.

Clara leapt onto the porch and ran into the house. With a flurry of movement, Momma swept Bessie roughly into her arms. Bessie whimpered.

Clara gasped in relief. Still alive!

"I know where you been," said Momma. Her eyes were tired and wild at the same time.

Clara licked her lips. Her mouth was dry as cotton. "Momma . . ."

"Don't *Momma* me."

"Old Sugar is outside, waiting to help."

"You go right back out and tell him to leave. Might as well have the devil himself in my house."

Clara didn't move. The light sound of Bessie's panting filled the room.

"Clara, I told you. Now *get!*" Momma stepped toward her, as if she could kick her back outside.

Clara wet her lips again, trying to figure out how to get past Momma's fear. "When we met him on Red Owl Mountain, he told us about his Auntie Charlotte Rose and how she worked the roots. He can help Bessie."

"He ain't touching Bessie." Momma lay her down on the big bed. "I see you ain't moving toward that door. All right, then, I can tell him myself."

"Momma, listen at me," Clara said. She stood between Momma and the door. She couldn't let Momma send Old Sugar away. "No matter what happened to your Momma, Old Sugar won't hurt Lil Bits. He only works a good hand."

"He told you that, did he? Hunh! If a hoodoo man puts a bad fix on you, your ghost goes moaning and tramping around this earth forevermore, and you never get to heaven. You want Bessie out there in the field every night, howling for you to come out in the dark with her? I spent years worrying my Momma was going to come back and haunt me."

Clara grabbed Momma by the shoulders. "There ain't nothing to fear from this hoodoo man." She was hollering at Momma and shaking her, and she didn't even care. "He wasn't the one who put a fix on your Momma!"

The dime was shining and bouncing around on Momma's neck, and then the next thing Clara knew, Momma took hold of her and threw her off to the side. Like Bessie would throw a rag doll. Clara was somehow still on her feet, but she wasn't between Momma and the door anymore.

Momma ran to the door and pulled it open. Like a shadow, Clara followed her onto the porch.

Old Sugar looked up at them from the path, his eyes sharp and bright. He was completely still.

Momma held the silver dime out in front of her like it was some kind of shield. "You ain't welcome here."

"You don't need that dime with me," said Old Sugar. His voice was soft.

"You do hoodoo?" Momma asked.

"I can undo evil fixes, but I never work them."

"How do I know you ain't lying?"

"I'm telling you God's truth. He must want to use my hands and His good medicines if He sent Clara to me, riding through the night."

Clara didn't think anyone had sent her. She had sent herself. But she felt something shift in Momma. Like the wind died down in a big storm. Sudden. Momma walked quickly off the porch and stood square in front of Old Sugar.

"What did you say?" she asked. "About the Lord?"

Old Sugar's forehead wrinkled up. Then he repeated, "I'm telling you God's truth."

"There. You said it again." Momma nodded. She started pacing back and forth in front of Old Sugar. She only went a short way, then she turned and went back, like an animal with its leg caught in a trap. Back and forth, back and forth.

Clara started down the stairs and then stopped.

"Alright, alright," Momma was muttering to herself, then shifted into prayer. "Oh Lord. You know my heart, Lord, you know my heart. I've done what I can for my baby; now you need to help me, Lord. I don't believe he could say Your name if he were following evil ways." Back and forth, back and forth.

She stopped in front of Old Sugar. Clara could see the muscles on Momma's neck standing out tight. "Alright," Momma said, "we'll take a chance on you."

She pushed her face right up to him. "But if I'm wrong, and you're a two-shadow man, I hope thunder and lightning strike you down dead." She turned and walked back to the house, passing Clara on the steps like she wasn't even there. Old Sugar followed close behind, carrying his tow sack. He glanced at Clara.

She gave a slight nod. They both knew Momma believed Old Sugar only because she needed so badly to believe him. But that was enough.

chapter thirteen

Inside, the house was warm. Old Sugar lay his tow sack on the floor and knelt down in front of Bessie.

"Hello, Lil Bits," he whispered. "I got some herbs for you. We just need to figure out which ones to use."

Momma sat next to Bessie on the bed while Old Sugar looked her over. Momma's eyes followed every move he made. Clara stood nearby and watched as he unwrapped the rags around Bessie's elbows and knees. Tiredness was washing through Clara like it would carry her away. And Momma had the cabin too hot. It was making everything swim. Maybe she could just sit down for a minute now that Old Sugar was here.

She shrugged off his coat and hung it on the back of a chair. A soft gray darkness crept into the sides of her eyes and kept moving, covering up everything except a long, narrow tunnel around Momma and Bessie and Old Sugar. She felt herself swaying and heard a faraway voice that sounded like her own say "Momma!"

"Sugarcake!" Momma jumped up and grabbed hold of Clara and set her in the rocking chair.

Momma told her to put her head down between her knees, and she did. When she sat back up, nothing was dark or swimming around anymore. She just felt dreamy and light. In her dreaminess, she thought the ocean inside her pink-and-tan shell had come pouring out and was murmuring all around her, rocking her, filling her up with sleepiness.

"You all right now, Sugarcake?"

"I'm fine, Momma," she said, wanting to slip back to that pink-and-tan place where the ocean was murmuring.

It wasn't more than a few minutes before Old Sugar stood up. Clara looked over at him in her dreaminess. Now he would make something for Bessie. Then Bessie would get better and she could go to sleep.

"I brought a whole sack full of herbs," said Old Sugar. "But the best medicine for her fever ain't in there."

Clara jumped up. The lulling, rocking feelings crashed down around her feet.

"It's growing right by the creek," Old Sugar continued.

"What . . ."

"I'll explain as we work. Now, you got something big we can boil up water in?" He held his arms out in a wide circle. "A washtub, maybe?"

"We got a cast-iron pig pot," Clara said. Her heart was pounding. What was he going to do?

"Where is the pot?"

"In the field. You walked past it getting to the barn. It's under an oil cloth."

Old Sugar nodded. "That'll do just fine," he said. "Fill it up with water, quick as you can." His voice was sharp, almost barking. "Then build a fire under it. We got to get the water boiling." He handed her a sulfur match from his tow sack.

Clara stuffed the match into her pocket and grabbed the tin bucket. It was about half-full. She ran to the field. The moon had crept across the sky. Soon it would fall behind the trees. There would be only starlight, and then dawn would come. Dawn, and Bessie would live or die.

Clara pulled the oil cloth off the pig pot and poured the half-full bucket of water in. It splashed down into the pot and seemed to disappear. She ran through Momma's garden to the spring box behind the house and drew up a big bucketful of cold water. The metal handle dug into the palm of her hand as she ran it back to the pig pot. Over and over again she filled the bucket and emptied it into the pig pot. All the while her mind was going in circles, twisting and leaping with the confusion of it all. Why did Old Sugar want the pig pot full of hot water?

When the pot was almost full, Old Sugar came out. He stood next to Clara as she poured another bucket in. They could see the reflection of the moon skitter crazily across the moving water.

"That's enough. We need to leave room for the willow," he said. "Now let's get the fire started. Where's your woodpile?"

"Alongside the house, on the far side," Clara said.

"I'll get the wood," said Old Sugar. "You start the fire."

Clara dropped to her knees and swept the ground with her fingers, gathering up twigs and small branches. She stuffed them under the pig pot. Then she took his match out and scratched it on a brick to light it. Nothing happened. She did it again, harder. With a puff of white smoke, the match burst into flame. Carefully, she held it under the pile until flames crackled up through the twigs.

Clara fed little sticks into the fire until it was going on its own, tiny orange-red flames dancing up around the bottom of the pot.

Old Sugar dropped an armful of kindling next to her. "Keep the fire going, hot as you can." He headed back to the woodpile.

Clara shoved more sticks underneath. Her back

hurt from lifting and bending and stooping and hauling. When the flames were strong, she pushed some kindling into the fire and stood up.

Old Sugar dropped a load of wood beside the pot. "That should be enough. Now we need to cut willow branches. We'll put them in the water and boil it up into a medicine bath for Bessie."

"Why can't she just drink the medicine?" Clara asked.

"It's so strong it would burn her stomach. The warm water will make her skin soft. The medicine will get in that way and work quickly."

Old Sugar pulled out his pocketknife and offered it to her. Silently, Clara took Granny's knife out of her pocket and showed him. They walked down to the willows lining the creek.

Clara stood on one of the gnarly old roots and opened Granny's knife. She reached up, pulled a branch down, and cut through it. Over and over again she cut the willow branches, until she had a big armful. She looked over to where Old Sugar was working and saw that he had an armful too.

Side by side, they walked back to the pig pot. The

fire had burned down some while they were at the creek. Clara pushed her branches into the pot. The water was warm, almost hot. Old Sugar handed her his armful of willow, and she put it in, then shoved two more pieces of wood under the pot.

As she stared at the flames, the moon slipped slowly behind the mountain. The stars shone out bright in the blackened sky.

Old Sugar disappeared and came back with a long stick to stir the willow water.

"Now?" asked Clara.

"By and by, child." His voice seemed to come from all directions in the starry darkness. "It needs a good boil."

"We've got to hurry." Steam was rising off the top of the water.

"Can't hurry now."

"But the night's passing." She couldn't bear to say that dawn must be getting near, as if saying it might hurry it along.

"If we don't boil it good, it won't work."

Clara tried to force more wood under the pot.

Old Sugar watched her struggle for a moment.

"The fire's alright, child. We just have to wait."

Clara stopped, letting the last piece of kindling fall beside her on the ground. She could just make out the willow branches rolling in the bubbling water.

"We need to let it boil awhile," said Old Sugar. "Soon as the fire dies down, you can take out the willow branches and add cold water. Just enough to make it warm, you understand? Not too cold, not too hot. Like a good bath. Then it'll be ready."

Clara stared at him. Why didn't *he* pull out the willow and add the cold water? Then they would know it was done right. Instead, he was telling her how to do it. She was just opening her mouth to ask him when Old Sugar turned and walked back to the house.

Alone under the starry sky, Clara understood. Here she'd been worrying over trusting Old Sugar, and now he was trusting her.

When she went back inside, Old Sugar was kneeling in front of the fireplace. A fragile peace hung in the air.

Momma was in the rocking chair, wiping Bessie

down with a wet rag. Wiping and wiping, as if she could just wipe away the sickness. She was singing to Bessie again, soft and low.

Hush child, hush,
Hush child, hush,
Somebody's calling your name,
Hush child, hush.

At least she wasn't singing "Pray On."

Clara stroked Bessie's hot cheek and said, "We're boiling up some willow water to make you better." Bessie didn't move but just lay there limp, breathing those shallow breaths.

"Hush, Clara," said Momma softly. "It's no use trying to talk to her."

Nothing to do now but wait. Clara went over to watch Old Sugar. He had a frying pan on the coals and a small sack of cornmeal next to him. He sprinkled some in the pan and sat stirring it.

As soon as it parched brown, he poured in water and stirred. He handed a cupful of the hot brown liquid to Clara. "Drink this," he said. "It'll pass the time. I'm going to sit with your Momma."

Clara took her tea out to the porch. She couldn't bear to look at Bessie. She was afraid she might start counting Bessie's breaths, afraid they would stop.

She must have dozed off because she jerked awake, spilling cold tea all over her leg. How long had she been asleep? The rooster crowed in the barn, calling out in the predawn grayness. Clara ran down to the pig pot. The fire had died down to coals.

She stuck her hand in. Quickly she pulled it back out. Her skin felt tight and tingly. The water was mighty hot.

Clara grabbed Old Sugar's long stirring stick. She dipped it in the water, snagged the willow, and pulled it up. The hot branches burned her hands as she grabbed them and threw them aside. Then she ran to the spring for water, thrusting her hands deep to cool the burning.

One bucket wasn't quite enough, so she added another half to the pig pot. Then the water felt soothing and warm. She threw the last half-bucket on the coals.

Clara dashed back into the house, barely stopping herself from hollering. "It's ready," she said breathlessly.

Momma stood up with Bessie in her arms, and Clara led them outside. They formed a circle around the pot.

"Put her in the water, Momma." Clara was nearly whispering now. Momma gave Bessie a kiss on her forehead and then slid her into the warm water. She kept her arms loosely around her, holding her head out of the water. Momma started swaying gently side to side, a moaning, humming sound coming from her.

Gradually Clara made out what she was humming. "We all gather at the river, the beautiful, the beautiful river." Well, it was a baptism. Her sister was either going into everlasting life or coming back to this one.

Bessie lay limp in the water, her arms floating by her sides. Her eyes were closed. If it wasn't for her chest going up and down, Clara wouldn't have known she was alive.

"When will it work, Old Sugar?" Clara asked.

"Fever like this takes some breaking," he said.

This felt like the hardest part of all. She stared at Bessie, lying in the pig-pot water while Momma held her. After awhile Clara slipped under the place of talking and thinking, and went to where all her feelings were. She stood so long waiting, even her feelings fell away, and finally there was only silence as deep as the whole starry sky.

The coming sun lit up the skimming clouds, turning them rosy and gold. Clara heard frogs calling back and forth down by the creek. The air felt cool and damp.

From the barn, the rooster crowed again.

There was a little splash in the pot.

"Lil Bits?" Momma said, so softly it was almost a sigh.

At first, there was no answer. Then Bessie made a tiny sound, like the mew of a newborn kitten.

"Gracious God almighty!" Momma gathered Bessie to her chest. Water ran off Bessie in tiny streams.

"Now, you just keep her in there awhile," Old Sugar said.

Bessie mewed again and looked at Momma with dull eyes. Then it seemed like her spirit rose up inside her, and she smiled.

"Oh, Lil Bits," Momma breathed, and this time there was pure happiness in her voice.

Momma slid Bessie back in the warm bath. The front of her dress was soaking wet. Tears streamed down her face as she rocked Bessie gently back and forth in the water.

Clara's knees started shaking, and she grabbed for the edge of the pig pot. "It worked, Old Sugar," she said, full of wonder.

" 'Course it did." Old Sugar laughed softly. "My Auntie Charlotte Rose was always right."

A wild, joyful feeling took hold of Clara. She threw out her arms and arched back on her toes. "We did it!" she called out to the sky.

When she dropped back on her heels, Momma

was staring at her with such a fierce and tender look it took Clara's breath away.

"You are a sent-God child," Momma said. "For true and true."

For a long time, nobody said anything, then Old Sugar spoke. "I believe your Momma's right, child."

chapter fourteen

Clara was walking up the path next to Momma. They had just dropped off a small bag of peppermints at Annie Mae's. Their breath made small puffs in the late afternoon air. Even the chill couldn't take the warmth out of Clara. They were bringing home the crock.

She could hear Buckshot's steady footsteps as he walked behind them, the new crock wrapped in a quilt and roped to his back. This one was darker than the others, with a wide blue stripe around the top and a big number 10 glazed on the side.

Clara stepped carefully, trying to stay out of the

muddy puddles from the rain last night. They'd had a few light freezes, and that cold mud could stick to your feet and chill you like nothing else. Daddy was making her a new pair of shoes for school, but until then she was watching where she walked.

She could feel Momma's eyes on her.

"For just a heartbeat you looked like Granny," said Momma. "I wonder when that started happening, without me noticing."

Maybe she was getting to be more like Granny on the inside, too, thought Clara. Riding a mule out into the starry night to go after a hoodoo man! "No telling what I might get up to next," she said, grinning at Momma.

"Hunh!"

"Momma—" Clara started, then stopped.

"Sugarcake?"

Clara swallowed. "Old Sugar wants to take me out herb gathering in the spring." She started talking faster, afraid Momma would interrupt. "He says there's lots of herbs to pick, once the frogs start croaking. Things like sassafras and chickweed and horseradish and Johnny-jump-up."

Clara took a deep breath and waited for Momma to say something, but Momma only gave a small nod.

They walked in silence. The sun slid behind the bare trees, and they lost the thin warmth it had given. Clara drew her coat tighter around her. Off in the woods, she spotted the glimmer of hundreds of persimmons. She'd forgotten all about them.

"Oh, look, Momma!" Clara pointed. "Soon as we get a killing frost, we can come back for the persimmons."

They stopped and stared at the tree. All the leaves had dropped off, and the dark orangy fruits hung in thick clusters on the long branches. Clara's mouth watered. Every one of those persimmons was going to be slippery soft and sweet as soon as that tree got frostbit.

Buckshot gently nudged the back of her head, his breath warm on her neck.

Clara looked at the light, wispy clouds overhead, slipping across the sunset-filled sky. No thick clouds blanketed the earth, holding back the cold. That frost might just come tonight. She reached up and gave Buckshot a good scratch behind his ears, right where he liked it. "Winter's coming," she whispered.

She could feel it sweeping in.

A Note from the Author

Clara Raglan was a real person. When I met her, she was in her eighties, short and round with two wispy gray braids pinned up on her head. Her knees hurt, and she walked with a rolling gait, trailing her fingers along the wall of the old Victorian house where she lived in San Francisco.

I had come to see if I could help her knees with acupuncture. When the first treatment brought down the swelling and lessened her pain, I began going to her house weekly. I would put six or eight thin needles in Clara's legs and arms while she lay on her bed. After the treatment, I would curl up in the big pink armchair in the corner of her bedroom, and she would tell me stories about her life.

When Clara was eighteen, she married and moved to San Francisco, where her husband ran a boot-black stand. Several years later her father died, and Bessie and Momma came to live with Clara and her husband. They were never apart again.

Clara didn't have any children of her own. But for twenty-eight years she worked for the Joneses, who had eleven children. "I raised 'em all up," Clara said matter-of-factly. Nine of the children remained in San Francisco as adults. They and their children were in and out of Clara's house constantly. Often three or four Joneses were there, cooking meals, talking on the phone, watching TV, or sewing on the old Singer sewing machine that had belonged to Momma.

"They're like my own kids," Clara explained with a grin. "Now, scat, all of you," she'd say once in a while, sending them away so she could have a little peace and quiet.

Clara loved to talk about her childhood. She told me about her granny who had been a slave on a big plantation in Georgia, and how she used to shout, "Glory, glory!" when she was excited. I heard about hoodoo and herbs and the woods that Clara loved. My favorite story was how she had saved her sister's life by boiling up willow in the pig pot. And whenever she finished telling a story, Clara would say, "Stepped on a pin, pin bent. That's the way the story went."

Momma lived to be ninety-five. Clara's husband and Bessie died first, and Clara's mother grew increasingly frail. After I had known Clara a few years, she let on that her mother's spirit still lived with her. Clara often talked with her and always had a sense of her presence. Momma was not a haunt but a good spirit, choosing to remain with Clara because of the love between them.

Clara lived into her early nineties. When any of us worried her by saying we were going to miss her after she died, she'd have none of it. "You don't go till your time comes," she'd say. "And when you go, you got to go of *something*."

For many years after Clara's death from a stroke, her stories lay quietly inside me. I was working as an acupuncturist and herbalist, and raising two small children. When I began writing, I wanted to share with others the willow-bath story.

I quickly found out I didn't know enough to turn Clara's story into a book. I headed for the library. At the University of California, a search through old photographs revealed hundreds of details about life during the turn of the century. I read stories told decades ago by African-Americans, written the way they were spoken. At the Library of Congress, I listened to *The Slave Narrative* tapes, recordings made in the 1930s and early 1940s of old people who had been slaves when they were young. I made several visits to Tennessee, to Conner Motlow and his daughter Lizzie, friends whose family had been farmers for over a hundred and fifty years. Listening to them talk about old-time farming brought back memories of my own lean years growing up on ten acres surrounded by cattle ranchers.

When Clara told me about the willow bath, I hadn't known why it had saved Bessie's life. I studied the uses of herbs in folk medicine. I found that willow bark has been used for several thousand years all over the world as a cure for fever, inflammation, and pain. At the end of the nineteenth century, it was synthesized in Europe and named aspirin. Today, Americans take sixteen thousand tons of aspirin each year—eighty million pills' worth!

In traditional Chinese medicine, ginseng is one of the best-known herbs. The wild ginseng is much stronger than farm-grown plants, so it has been hunted all over the world for centuries. As early as the 1700s, ginseng was gathered throughout the forests of the United States and Canada by Native Americans, explorers, and settlers.

Today about one-fourth of our modern Western drugs are based on plants. For example, digitalis—used for heart problems—comes from foxglove. And more drugs are being discovered all the time in plants. Recently we've begun using a drug called Taxol in the treatment of cancer. It's found in the bark of the Pacific or Western yew tree.

I let all this information—cultural, historical, and medical—settle down in me with Clara's story. After a while, I began creating scenes and dialogue to make her story grow into a book. And as I worked, I found my way back to Clara as a child, full of longings and dreams, struggles and joys. Some of them are hers; some I have imagined. But I hope they all are true to her nature and her times.

Stepped on a pin,
pin bent.
That's the way
the story went.

Elizabeth Partridge was the first person to graduate with a degree in Women's Studies from the University of California at Berkeley. After earning a licentiate of acupuncture in 1978, she became one of the few Caucasians practicing Chinese medicine in the United States. One of the author's patients in San Francisco was Clara Raglan, an African-American woman in her eighties. Clara told Elizabeth the stories of her rural upbringing in Tennessee. Elizabeth's favorite story was how Clara saved her sister's life using a folk-medicine cure.

Elizabeth has produced a film and edited a book on her godmother, photographer Dorothea Lange. *Clara and the Hoodoo Man* is her first novel.

Visit her web site at:
http://www.partridge.org